Lords of the Var

THE PLAYFUL PRINCE

By

Michelle M. Pillow

Futuristic Romance

New Concepts   Georgia

Be sure to check out our website for the very best in fiction at fantastic prices!

When you visit our webpage, you can:
* Read excerpts of currently available books
* View cover art of upcoming books and current releases
* Find out more about the talented artists who capture the magic of the writer's imagination on the covers
* Order books from our backlist
* Find out the latest NCP and author news--including any upcoming book signings by your favorite NCP author
* Read author bios and reviews of our books
* Get NCP submission guidelines
* And so much more!

We offer a 20% discount on all new Trade Paperback releases ordered from our website!

Be sure to visit our webpage to find the best deals in e-books and paperbacks! To find out about our new releases as soon as they are available, please be sure to sign up for our newsletter (http://www.newconceptspublishing.com/newsletter.htm) or join our reader group (http://groups.yahoo.com/group/new_concepts_pub/join)!

The newsletter is available by double opt in only and our customer information is *never* shared!

Visit our webpage at:
www.newconceptspublishing.com

New Concepts Publishing, Inc.
5202 Humphreys Rd.
Lake Park, GA 31636

ISBN 1-58608-842-4
© May 2005 Michelle M. Pillow
Cover art (c) copyright 2006 Eliza Black

NCP books are available at special quantity discounts for bulk purchases for sales promotions, premiums, fund raising, or educational use. For details, write, email, or phone New Concepts Publishing, Inc., 5202 Humphreys Rd., Lake Park, GA 31636; Ph. 229-257-0367, Fax 229-219-1097; orders@newconceptspublishing.com.

First NCP Trade Paperback Printing: October 2006

Dedication:
To Katie, for your enthusiasm and spirit.

"A man cannot bow to a woman and still call himself a man." - King Attor of the Var

Chapter One

Tori Elliot, the very dignified scientist, opened her mouth. Her heart beat furiously in her chest, thumping so hard it echoed in her ears. For a moment, no sound left her as she kept her eyes focused straight ahead. There was a dramatic pause and all around her was dead silence. Suddenly, the twentieth century earth music picked up and her naked body jerked into movement. She belted out the tune into her mouth sanitizer turned microphone with her mirror as audience. After a few bars, she dropped the mouth sanitizer and danced and sang around her metal cabin. Her arms flung through the air, wild and carefree, as she slowly got dressed.

The spaceship she was on belonged to the Exploratory Science Commission. The ESC hired out staff and freelance scientists to large corporations, mostly contracting ecological work with mining companies and wealthy environmentalist groups. The ship had been traveling through deep space for weeks, just now reaching the outer edge of the Y quadrant.

Tori didn't really care where they were. Her last job, testing mineral compounds fourteen thousand feet below the ice surface of Sintaz, had been a great success. With the bonus the drilling company had given her, she'd made enough space credits to support herself in high style for at least a couple years. She was going to take that money and have a month long spa treatment on Quazer while she figured out her next move.

The material of the black, skintight jumpsuit stretched as she pushed her arms into it. The outfit molded to her body, covering her arms and legs completely. Even though she didn't technically work for ESC, but was a freelancer, she was expected to dress in uniform when contracted through them. They all came with a transmitter sewn into the v-neckline, so the company could find them if anyone went missing. There was always a certain amount of risk in what she did, but the scientific rewards were well worth it. Besides, she never took unnecessary chances.

"Dr. Elliot."

"Ah! Crap!" Tori jumped. The earth music was automatically turned off as the voice invaded her privacy. Turning to the round cabin mirror, she quickly smoothed down her wild hair and threw it over her shoulders. She stood, watching the shiny surface. It glimmered slightly, fading into a view screen. Her reflection was replaced by the ship's senior ESC advisor, Dr. Fontaine.

"Good Morning, Dr. Fontaine," Tori answered, keeping a rigidly professional expression. Her heart skittered around in her chest from being frightened in the middle of her impromptu dance number. That was the last thing she wanted her colleagues seeing.

"Is everything all right, Dr. Elliot?" Fontaine asked. He was an older man with graying black hair. He wore the black jumpsuit of the company covered by a white lab coat. Tori hadn't had much contact with him on Sintaz, as he stayed up on the surface while she went below ground with her crew. "You look flushed."

"I was logging in my fitness hours early." Tori dutifully answered. Okay, so it was a stretch of the truth, but she had worked up a sweat. Besides, she really hated logging in fitness hours.

"Ah, quite right," Fontaine answered, easily dismissing his question. "Listen, we have a minor situation. The Human Intelligence Agency is coming aboard to commandeer our ship. They've asked that all personnel records be turned over to them immediately and we have complied. They have assured us that this should only delay travel for a few days at most."

"What does the HIA want with a bunch of scientists?" Tori asked, mildly concerned. "Do they suspect something on board?"

"I don't have all the details, doctor, but they seemed most insistent that it's an intergalactic emergency. They've requested you to head up the team."

"Wait, what team?" Tori demanded. Damn it! She was on vacation as of last assignment's completion. She wasn't ready to take another job so soon. Besides, she hadn't signed a contract with ESC. They couldn't force her to do anything! Keeping her voice level, she said, "I'm not personnel. Why were my private records handed over? As of the completion of my last mission, I'm technically a civilian passenger."

"Sorry, doctor, they had an intergalactic warrant. We had no choice but to give them the qualifications of all onboard scientists." Fontaine's expression gave nothing away, but she didn't expect it to.

If the HIA wanted her to head up a team, she knew she'd have to head up the team. They might pay her, but she wasn't happy about being forced to do a job. Technically, she'd be given a 'choice', but if she refused they could make the rest of her career a nightmare. When they were done with her, she'd be lucky to get work teaching school children scientific categorizing on some remote planet.

Well, Fontaine said it was only a few days delay so it shouldn't be that bad. They probably had a liquid ore tanker ship crash in an isolated area or some other type of ecological disaster. Why else would they need her? Her specialties were alien biology and geology. Remaining professionally calm, she stated, "Very well, Dr. Fontaine. Please inform me when they arrive. I'd like to be briefed on my new assignment as soon as possible so I can prepare."

"Thank you, doctor," Fontaine said. "Your willingness is noted and appreciated."

"Doctor," Tori said, nodding. The mirror blipped and she was once more alone with her reflection. Under her breath, she hissed, "Willingness my ass!"

What did the HIA want with her? She didn't feel like working. She needed a break--a long, relaxing vacation in a place that didn't have artic temperatures all year round.

Tori sighed, her good humor dampened by the turn of events. The music started again where it'd left off, but she was no longer in the mood. Irritated, she called, "Music off. Bed."

The music turned off and a narrow bed slid out of the metal wall of the cabin. She threw herself down on the stiff mattress with a thud. Groaning heavily, she stared at the metal ceiling in dejection.

With a grumble, she turned her back on the room, facing the metal wall. "So much for my time off."

* * * *

"This is the planet of Qurilixen," Franklin, as he told Tori to call him, said. He pointed to a 3-D map floating above the desk. The small, transparent red sphere rotated slowly between them. There weren't many bodies of water that she could see, but there was a mountain range and plenty of forest area. It was quite possible the dense forest hid rivers and swampland. By the apparent height of the trees, she'd guess they were surrounded by excessive moisture.

Franklin was a mission director with the HIA. According to him she was now a temporary HIA employee and he was her new temporary boss. His shortly cropped, dark brown hair was trimmed to militant perfection and he walked with rigid purpose. He was young for a director, but that didn't stop him from ordering those around him about with confidence.

Tori had met his kind before--all work, no play. Not that there was anything wrong with that. She was the same way while on the job--okay, mostly she was.

"And here," Franklin continued, his hip perched on the edge of the desk, as he pointed at the floating sphere, "is the Var palace. This is where we'll land and make contact with my agent."

"Excuse me, sir," Tori interrupted. She looked at the map and then at him. "But what, exactly, are we landing on Qurilixen for? I need to choose and brief a team, pack my supplies, work on securing permits. In order to do all that, I need to know what we're up against."

"Everything you need has already been assembled for you, Dr. Elliot. As for your team, you will command every scientist on board this ship for the duration of this mission." Franklin paused and Tori instantly filled the silence.

"But, there are nearly a hundred scientists on this ship, maybe more. You can't mean me to command them all."

"Yes, I do," he stated easily, as if it was an everyday occurrence to be handed a huge, career breaking assignment such as this one.

Tori swallowed. Even if it was for only a few days, the fact that the HIA picked her out of hundreds to handle their "intergalactic emergency" would do volumes for her record, not to mention her pay demand. She tried not to be nervous. She couldn't mess this up--whatever it was. She wondered which part of her work record had impressed them. The biological categorizing on Denat 7? The time she was second in command and helped clean up the mineral spill on Merca? Her numerous publications on DNA sequencing and its application to modern exploratory science?

"It's a simple assignment and you'll be afforded with the best equipment and protective gear the HIA has to offer." Franklin smiled at her, but the look hardly passed as pleasant. "I will offer you whatever assistance I can. All we ask is that you be quick and efficient. I want you in and out of there fast. Discretion is a very vital key in this matter."

Tori hid her smile. How discreet was sending down a hundred scientists to a primitive planet?

"And what would that 'simple' assignment be?" she insisted.

"One of our agents has detected biological weaponry from Ranoz. They believe to have found the weapon intact. It will be your job to test the Var palace and everyone who's come in contact with that crate to see if they have been contaminated. It will also be your job to make sure the situation is contained." Franklin again paused and Tori wondered if he was doing it for dramatic effect. It really wasn't necessary. What he said was dramatic enough on its own. "You'll have the team down with you for one day. I expect you to utilize them efficiently and get the job done in that time."

Tori nodded, already making a chain of command list in her head. "Is that all?"

"No," Franklin continued. "After one day the majority of scientists will be coming back on board. We'd like you to stay behind with a team of no more than three. We need you to run a scan of the surrounding marshland to see if there is anything my agent might have missed. I estimate it should only take a little over a month to test the surrounding area."

Tori listened to him with astonishment. "You're joking. I was told the assignment was only for a few days. I don't have time for--"

"I never joke about something so serious," Franklin answered sternly. Tori doubted the man joked about anything. "And ESC assures me you aren't due anywhere else. They said you refused to sign another contract and were planning to take a vacation. I'd say saving lives takes precedence over those plans, Dr. Elliot. I took the liberty of canceling your hotel room on Quazer and all flight plans.

Refunds have been credited to your account, as well as a hefty HIA advance for doing this. I suggest you volunteer for the assignment, Dr. Elliot. If we have to force you to do it, you won't get paid."

Tori frowned. Those were lovely options. Do it and get paid, do it and don't get paid. In her head she laughed sarcastically, but she didn't dare make a sound to him.

"But ... why me?" She asked, confused. "I've never dealt with a biological weapons threat before. I specialize in chemical spills and environ tests. I think there has been a mistake. Surely there is someone else on board more qualified to handle--"

"There is, but you have unique qualifications we feel will help in this particular situation. We want you in charge." Franklin stood, looking uncomfortable. He reached over, picking up an electronic clipboard. He pushed a button and began to look over her file. "Your record as a scientist is impeccable and you are qualified in the fields we need for this particular assignment. Your records state that you are a leading authority on physical geography and biogeography, not to mention your experience in a wide array of areas-- atmospheric sciences, chemistry, oceanography, physics, botany, and microbiology. We also feel your background in bio--"

"Yes," Tori interrupted. "I'm well aware of my field of study. I don't really need my educational past and work history read for me. What I do need to know is what exactly my unique qualifications are that would make me the best candidate for *this* job."

Franklin cleared his throat and set the clipboard on the desk. He hit the button to draw down the 3D map. The red sphere disappeared.

"Director?" she insisted when he was quiet.

"How much do you know about Qurilixen?" Franklin rubbed the bridge of his nose.

"Not much," Tori admitted. "I don't think I've even heard it mentioned before today."

"Qurilixen is a planet predominately of males. Due to the blue radiation of one of their threes suns, it's nearly genetically impossible for them to produce female children. There are two main races--the Var, who we will be in contact with, and the Draig. Both are monarchies." Franklin lifted a paper folder off his desk and handed it to her. "Here, I had intelligence put this together for you. Since this planet is not part of the intergalactic treaty, we don't have much else to go on. But, we've had an agent working on the planet for several months and are assured the Var will be cooperative in our efforts. What we do have on them will be in there. I suggest you read it over carefully."

Tori nodded once and tucked the folder under her arm.

"We need you to get a scientific proposal ready to present to the Var king and any other officials there might be. As I said, they aren't a part of the intergalactic treaty. It would be best for all concerned if we got permission to check their marshes and caves first. It would severely decrease the risk to anyone poking around down there to have that permission. I'll be blunt. If we have to do this covertly, we will, but the life risk greatly increases."

"Namely for me," she said.

"Yes, doctor, namely for you and any with you."

"Is there reason to believe this is hostile territory?" she asked, keeping her voice calm, though inside she was tense with nerves.

"I honestly don't know. If there is, they're territorial skirmishes, isolated to the planet itself." Franklin cleared his throat, boldly meeting her gaze. "Stay neutral and don't take sides."

"I still don't understand how that makes me qualified for this," Tori said, pulling the folder from beneath her arm. She looked at the cover stamped top secret, but didn't open it. "I'm not trained for hostile territory and know very little about intergalactic negotiations. Wouldn't you need someone with a political background for this?"

"It's simple, Dr. Elliot." Franklin did his best not to grin, but she could see the humor in his eyes.

Great, now he decides to get a sense of humor, she thought.

"They're a planet of men," Franklin continued. "And you're the youngest, most attractive, most qualified female scientist we have."

* * * *

Advanced scientific study since she could read, a doctorate in two scientific fields by the time she was twelve and several masters in many others since that time, ten years of intense on-the-job experience, countless brain uploads, and here she was reduced to being pimped out by the HIA because she was a woman. If her Galaxy Playmate sister, 'Sapphire', ever found out about this, she'd never hear the end of it. It was just too humiliating for words.

"Oh, this is too good," Tori mumbled. "They lose some stupid government weapon and I'm reduced to simpering and flirting with a bunch of savages so they can make sure they got it all back."

Tori took a drink of wine and looked down at the contents of the "top secret" folder she'd been given. Most of the photographs were aerial views taken from a satellite. There were a few pages of specs about the planet's surface, some graphs of atmospheric readings, and miscellaneous notes about the weather and culture. All of it was pretty basic and made her wonder just how intelligent the HIA "intelligence" really was.

Tori snorted, reaching down to the floor to empty the wine bottle into her glass. She was well on her way to getting drunk, but didn't care. They weren't arriving on Qurilixen until the next morning and she'd have plenty of time to sleep it off.

The Var were a race of shape-shifting cats. Apparently, not much was really known about them, but that they were in the process of negotiating peace with the Draig--their shape-shifting dragon neighbors. The Qurilixian in general were classified as a warrior class that had many petty territorial skirmishes that broke out every fifteen or so years between the rival kingdoms.

The best comparison anyone could make is that the men were like the barbaric warriors of medieval earth. Both races worshipped many gods and favored natural comforts to modern technological conveniences. Intelligence assumed, from the concentrated areas of cropland and cow-like animal herds to the far north and south, that they preferred to raise, grow, and cook their own food.

Tori sighed, pushing the papers away. None of the information was really helpful to her. Unless, she was to assume by barbaric society, they would be easily swayed by batting eyelashes and wiggling hips. What in the world did she know about flirting? She wasn't ugly, but she'd never be voted Galaxy Playmate of the year like her bimbo of a sister either. When Sapphire was learning to put on makeup, she'd been building model quasars and performing scientific tests while restructuring their density.

"Medieval earth," she mused, kicking the folder and contents off her bed with her bare foot as she lay down. Reaching over the side of the bed, she placed the wine glass on the floor. "Not exactly a flattering description--disease, ignorance, superstition, bad hygiene, missing teeth, boils, pockmarks...."

Tori continued mumbling her long list, as she closed her eyes. The mental image she had of the Qurilixian people wasn't exactly flattering. She was used to dealing with corporate business types and other scientists, not superstitious peasants. In her mind, she decided to recap what she learned from the thin file.

The Var palace was a magnificent structure, dominating the surrounding Var city in the valley beneath it. According to the human women who had come to live in the palace over the centuries, it reminded them of the basic structure of the medieval castles found long ago on earth, with an old Moroccan blend to the architectural design.

The Var people were skilled craftsmen and it showed. Since a Var man would live for hundreds of years, they had a lot of time to perfect their skills. Inside, the palace had fantastically hand-woven rugs for the floors and beds. The beautiful inlaid tile walls were of intricate symmetrical patterns. The tiles showcased an exceptional display of colors--blue, red, orange, gold, green. The arched doorways were carved to perfection and great detail.

But, not only was the palace beautiful, it was functional. The halls were like a maze and it was easy for those not familiar with them to get lost. The mainframe computer was engineered into every room and hall, even the center courtyard the family used for privacy. Siren, the mainframe's programmed name, could answer questions, read life functions, open doors, prepare food--anything a busy Var prince might need. With the right level of security clearance, a person could even order Siren to locate anyone on the grounds or alert the palace guards. It was here in this lush, cushy paradise that the five Var princes grew up.

The oldest, Kirill, was now king. He was recently named ruler after the death of his father, King Attor. Next in line was Falke, the Commander of the Guards. Reid was Commander of the Outlands and also had a twin brother named....

Tori frowned and sat up. Looking over the side of the bed, she saw the paper she was looking for and picked it up. Scanning her eyes over the sheet in the dim light, she read, "Twin brother named Jarek, personality and situation unknown."

She dropped the paper and lay back down. The twins were the only princes with the same mother. Jarek was in space so she didn't have to worry about him.

"Lovely culture," she mused, chuckling drunkenly. "Okay, Tori, focus. The more facts you know, the better prepared you are."

Prince Quinn, the youngest of the Var brothers, was the ambassador. Ambassadors, in her experience, were usually bores--ugly, boring, tediously pompous bores.

"Hmm, Prince Quinn. Well, being as I'm a foreigner, I'll probably have to deal with you," Tori mumbled thoughtfully. "Let's just hope you have some semblance of manners, shall we?"

Tori snorted, laughing to herself. She closed her eyes, really close to falling asleep. Her mind swirled with the pleasant numbness of liquor.

"Mmm, let's just hope you know how to bathe."

Chapter Two

Prince Quinn of the Var smiled playfully at the lovely woman next to him. Leaning his face forward, he nuzzled her cheek with his light, seductive kisses, flicking his tongue out over her skin until she shivered. "I told you the king was in love. He'll not take any other mistresses. I'm sorry, Linzi, but you'll just have to look elsewhere."

"Elsewhere, like here?" Linzi giggled. She smiled prettily, as her hand went straight for Quinn's large erection. Impishly batting her dark eyelashes at the handsome prince, she stroked him through his clothes. Her look was of pure invitation, making it clear that she was more than ready to meet the young prince's desires right then and there in the palace hallway. She licked her lips and tilted her mouth up to his in offering.

Quinn chuckled. Linzi was a beautiful woman and luckily he didn't have the same problem as his older brother Kirill. Kirill was in love with his mistress, an undercover agent for the Human Intelligence Agency. If Kirill played his hand right, Ulyssa would soon be his queen and he would be life mated to one woman for the rest of his days--giving her the ability to live just as long as he.

Linzi stroked him harder when he didn't immediately take her offered lips. Quinn's look darkened, becoming devilishly mischievous in its intent as he leaned in for a kiss. His fingers lifted to cup a firm breast, causing the woman to moan. He had no such plans for life mating to one woman. He liked being carefree. He liked playing around, having fun. Marriage didn't sound like much fun to him. Besides, what was it his father had always said?

"Women are like fruit on the vine, each piece sweeter than the first. Why sample one, when you can sample them all?"

Quinn moaned lightly. If he played his hand right, Linzi would soon be pressed against the palace wall fulfilling his very masculine desires. He deepened his kiss, thrusting his tongue boldly past her lips.

"Excuse me, sir, could you tell me where--*Oh, good God in heaven!*"

Quinn pulled back from Linzi's lips and whispered, "Just a moment, sweetheart. Don't go anywhere."

Linzi giggled. She was pressed against the wall by Quinn's body so she couldn't move if she wanted to. By the look on her face, she definitely didn't want to.

Smiling, the prince tilted back just far enough to see the bearer of the mortified voice. Quinn wasn't too surprised to see it was a female scientist. HIA scientists were crawling all over the palace, checking to make sure everyone was all right and not contaminated.

His father, King Attor, had ordered a biological weapon from the Medical Mafia, storing it in a cave in the swamplands. Undercover HIA Agent Ulyssa Payne, Kirill's mistress, discovered it. With the combined help of the Var and Draig royal houses, they managed to retrieve the weapon so that the HIA could take it off Qurilixen. The fact that the Draig, their ancient enemies, had banded together to help them was a great historical moment. Attor had always strove to conquer the Draig, but his last act in buying the biological weapon just might cause the two houses to find peace. It forced the Draig and Var to work together, to trust each other with their loved ones lives.

The Draig princes and their wives were now guests at the palace and had stayed to make sure the weapon really did leave. No one wanted the weapon left on the planet and they were all more than happy to see it go. If part of it going meant dealing with a bunch of scientists, so be it. It was better to get checked out, instead of not knowing until it was too late that the palace had been contaminated.

The woman scientist averted her gaze to the side, frowning in disapproval. Linzi pulled her hand off his arousal and rested it instead on his arm. Quinn stayed were he was, not moving his palm from her breast. He had nothing to be embarrassed about. Sex was as natural to his people as breathing. Besides, the doctor had wandered into his private hall.

"Can I help you?" he asked politely, as if he'd been caught staring at a cloud in the blue-green Qurilixen sky and not pawing a disheveled woman.

He didn't think it was possible, but the scientist's tanned features flushed a darker shade of red. She glanced at the floor then back at the wall. Her fingers clutched at the electronic clipboard she carried. Quinn finally let go of Linzi when he saw the woman wasn't even tempted to glance back at them. He grinned. There was no point in continuing a show if there was no longer an audience.

"I'll see you later, my lord," Linzi said softly. Quinn barely paid her any notice as she went running down the hall toward the palace harem where she lived. She'd been one of King Attor's women, though she'd never actually slept with the dead king, but was merely a forgotten member of his once massive collection. When their father died in battle against the Draig, Kirill had urged the women to find husbands and leave the palace. Many had done so happily. Those that were left were still technically looking for mates. However, until that day came they were more than happy to bide their time in the harem, flirting and sleeping with the handsome, rich princes.

The scientist didn't readily speak as Linzi disappeared around the corner. Quinn stepped back from the wall and crossed his arms over his chest. Now that he was closer, he was afforded a better view of her. She was by no means too slender and reedy, but neither was she too plump. The lush curves of her body called to his hands. His palms itched to touch her, to test her womanly softness. Her rounded hips, her larger breasts--breasts made to smother a man's face in pleasure. Quinn didn't think it was possible, but his erection lurched and became harder--painful in its size and need.

The scientist took a deep breath and struggled with her words. Finally, she stated, "I'm looking for Prince Quinn. I was told he was in this direction."

Quinn smiled. The woman again clutched nervously at an electronic clipboard in her hands, working her fingers along the sides. Letting his voice dip, he said, "I'm Quinn."

"You...?" She blinked in surprise, turning her dark eyes up to him. She assessed him in a cold manner that actually did nothing to hamper his arousal. If anything, he became more excited by it. "You can't possibly be ... I mean ... you are ... a prince?"

Her words trailed off as her eyes finally traveled down to his protruding groin. A strange squeaking noise sounded in the back of her throat. Quinn grinned, sniffing the air. The sudden pouring of feminine interest emanated from her thighs and he smelled the distinct perfume of her desire, her unmistakable lust. It called to him. Before he knew what he was doing, he stepped forward and reached for her.

* * * *

Tori had been stunned to find Prince Quinn making out with a woman in the hall for all to see, but she couldn't say she was terribly surprised. His "girlfriend" didn't seem as proud to be caught in public and Tori watched as the woman practically tripped to get away from them.

Tori took a calming breath, quietly assessing the prince. He was a handsome man with bright blue eyes that sparkled with unmistakable mischief. He was young too--much younger than any ambassador she'd ever seen. His body was slender yet unquestionably toned. Even motionless, she could tell he'd move with the liquid grace of his kind.

There was something slow and seductive in the way the Var carried themselves--like hunters crouched, stalking their prey, ready to attack. They truly were like wild cats.

His shirt appeared to be one piece of material, with two narrow straps over the shoulders. The shirt was held together by black cross lacing beneath his arms, leaving his muscled sides and waist exposed. His pants were of the same material as the shirt, soft, yet molding to his firm, delicious body. A belt clung around his narrow waist. More lacing made its way down to his knees, over the outside length of his thighs, leaving no indention of firm muscle to the imagination, as it revealed tanned flesh. The muscles along his hip flexed erotically as he shifted his weight and a seductive dimple formed. She gripped the clipboard, itching to reach forward, to push into the laced opening of his pants to feel his taut flesh for herself.

Her eyes were drawn to his hips, moving along his narrow waist. Suddenly, they stopped. Between his thighs towered the most massive protrusion she'd ever seen on a man. Her mouth went dry. Her body instantly responded, tingling with warmth and desire. The ESC jumpsuit became strangely constricting on her flesh, causing her nipples to bud up from her breasts. She became hot, nearly sweating. Moisture pooled between her thighs, making ready for him. She was thankful she wore the white lab coat so that the violent reaction was hidden. Unaware of the act, she tugged the front of the coat closer together.

Tori had always been a sexually charged person, but she normally took care of matters herself. Her professional life didn't leave too many openings for finding lovers. When isolated with the same people for months at a time, it often wasn't wise to start an affair. Someone always ended up getting jealous, competition over her would ensue since she was often the only female, and fights would start. However, if she did have an affair, it was always with someone on her academic level and they were always, *always* discreet about it. A wave of disgust came over her as she thought of this savage making out for all to see--and he was a prince at that!

Shameful. Totally and utterly shameful.

His sudden movement caught her attention and she realized he stepped toward her. He lifted his hand, as if to touch her. Tori flinched and took a step back.

"Sir," Tori stammered. "I mean, my ... ah?"

"Quinn," he supplied with a rakish smile.

"Yes, my Quinn ... wait, no." She took another step back as he moved aggressively forward. The look on his face made her heart flutter in excitement.

"Your Quinn?" he mused in a low tone that sent chills over her spine. "You wish for me to be your Quinn?"

"Stop!" she demanded holding out her hand. He paused in his quest to get to her and grinned, waiting. Tori swallowed, nervous and distracted. "Prince Quinn. I am Dr. Elliot with ESC ... well, actually the HIA, well, not really, technically with HIA or ESC except--"

Was she babbling? Tori was pretty sure she sounded like she was babbling. Scientists didn't babble. It wasn't appropriate. Her scowl deepened. Oh, why was he continuing to look at her like that?

"Well, Dr. Elliot not technically with the HIA or ESC," Quinn said, lowering his jaw as he leaned forward. "I'm H-O-R-N-Y and you're extremely pretty."

"H-O...? Oh! Really!" Tori gasped, dismayed. She shook her head in disapproval.

"What? You're really so surprised? Can you blame me, Dr. Elliot? You were staring quite intently at--" Quinn began to motion down, acting as if their conversation was an everyday topic.

Tori held up her hand and shook her head frantically to stop him. Taking a deep breath, she centered her thoughts and made a silent promise to never drink the night before a big assignment again. Surely that was why her heart was pounding so hard and why her limbs were shaking. Swallowing, she forced her voice to rigid calmness. "Is there someone I could talk to about gaining permission to search the cave systems that the biological weapons were discovered in? The HIA has requested that I clear the cave and surrounding area of any and all contamination threats."

Someone other than you, she thought, not caring if he saw her distaste for his lewdness.

Quinn's smile faded and to her surprise, he turned serious. "You think something else is up there?"

"I'm honestly not sure. The recovered weapon appears to be intact and contains enough chemical to wipe out at least five planets. From that bit of information, I would deduce there was only the one, unless the caves were being used as a storage unit of some kind, which, given the political climate of your kingdom, isn't likely the case. From what I understand, your father was fighting a war with...."

Tori stopped, realizing that she might be speaking too candidly. That's why she hated being in political situations. Facts were facts and she was used to stating them, regardless of their popularity. In her job, facts were all that mattered. In politics, a person was supposed to say things diplomatically, twisting the words into just the right phrase. It was a skill she lacked. She looked up at the prince. His face hadn't changed. She swallowed nervously. He motioned his hand slightly for her to continue, not looking at all offended by her words.

Weakly, Tori said, "My checking would simply be a wise safety precaution for everyone concerned, especially your people. It won't cost you a thing, if that's your concern. HIA is taking care of my and the other scientists' salaries."

Quinn nodded, a motion she hoped was agreement.

"My team has nearly gotten through with the palace inhabitants and so far everyone has tested negative. I believe they're about finished." Tori looked at her clipboard and pretended to scan through the data. This man unnerved her. She couldn't concentrate on what she was saying to him. Was she repeating herself? Was he even listening? Did she tell him yet that they were about done testing the palace inhabitants? She thought it, but did she say it? Damn, he had the most brilliant blue eyes she'd ever seen in her life. Delicately clearing her throat, she said, "But, we'd still like to do a thorough scan of the caves. There is no point in us leaving anything behind."

Quinn seemed to contemplate her words. Tori lowered her voice and stepped closer. He didn't move, except for those blue eyes. They followed her, keeping fixed on her face.

Getting excited, Tori forgot her nervousness as she admitted in a secretive whisper, "There was also something else. I took the liberty of analyzing the strange dark mud on the biological weapon's crate. I believe it's from your marshes because I found some fresh moss that leads me to believe it wasn't already on the crate when it was brought here. Anyway, there was an extremely high level of what appears to be DTH12 compound, which I'm sure isn't indigenous to this particular planet, being as your swamp soil is classified as GR13H and not TDH14. What doesn't make sense is that DTH12 is primarily found in the slime trail of northeastern yellow slugs on the planet of Fluk in the H... What? Are you laughing at me?"

Quinn was indeed chuckling. Shaking his head, he said, "Woman, I have no idea what you just said."

Tori frowned. She should have known. Sarcastically, she drawled, "Your mud is neat and I'd like to look at it."

Okay, maybe that was a tad too condescending. Quinn grimaced but didn't appear overly offended. Lucky for her, because he might just be the man she had to impress.

Damn politics!

Noticing she'd drawn closer to him, she stepped back and regained a professional distance. Her face became hard and emotionless. "Who would I need to ask to get permission to set up camp within the marshes near the cave systems? I believe it is Var land and would first need whatever permits your kingdom requires before starting a scientific study of the geological features and surrounding wildlife, otherwise I'll never be able to apply for later funding if I find anything worth studying. The way I look at it, I can do my research and clear the caves at the same time. I can personally guarantee that we won't be a bother to anyone."

"Hmm, for that, you'd best seek an audience with the king. He'll be the one to give final approval since the cave systems are on Lord Myrddin's land," Quinn answered. The grin reappeared on his playful mouth and she doubted he ever took anything seriously. "Now, about this attraction between us."

Tori's frown deepened and Quinn's grin widened. His bright blue eyes glinted good-naturedly.

"Prince Quinn," she opened her mouth to give him a piece of her mind, only stopping as she remembered her goal was to be allowed to stay on the planet.

Tori hadn't been lying when she said the marshland mud was thoroughly interesting to her as a scientist. Though at the moment she hated her sense of civic duty, she did want to make sure the cave systems were clear. She wouldn't be able to live with herself if she found out ten years from now everyone on the planet died because she'd lipped off to an insufferably roguish prince and got kicked off the planet.

In her most professional tone, she said, "Thank you for your time. I'm sure your," Tori waved her hand in the direction of the hall where his girlfriend had disappeared, "royal duty calls."

"Dr. Elliot." Quinn's head dipped forward slightly.

She could tell he was going to say more, so instead, she hurriedly nodded back and stated, "Good day."

Tori turned on her heels and rushed down the hall to get away from him.

Quinn watched the woman stalk away from him and smiled. The lovely scientist was definitely a strange character. Chuckling, he walked after her at a slower pace. It was clear she wanted him. The smell of her longing was in his head, teasing him. He hadn't expected her to fall into his arms, but that didn't stop him from teasing. She was so serious, so flustered, that he just couldn't help himself. The fact that she resisted him made him desire her more.

Quinn's grin widened, trying to see her figure through the sway of the baggy lab coat. Feeling lighthearted, he began to whistle and he made his way to the main hall to join his brothers.

* * * *

The banquet hall was a splendid affair with a high domed ceiling of glass that let in the diffused light of the three suns. Long tables and bench seats were along the floor for group dining. At the front of the hall, on a raised platform, was the king's table. Tori took a deep breath, too tired to look at the mosaic pattern on the walls or the lovely tiled floor. She'd been working since before dawn--drawing blood samples, coordinating lab reports and scientists, overseeing tests on the biological weapon they now had safely stored on the HIA ship. It had been a long day, and would be an even longer evening. She'd be lucky to get to bed before midnight.

Taking a deep breath, she smoothed her dark hair back into her bun, hoping she looked professional. At least she'd been able to get out of the white protective gear they'd worn on arrival. She hated contamination suits. The plastic helmet and stiff gloves made it hard to move around in a laboratory environment.

King Kirill was at his table, but he wasn't alone. Prince Reid and Prince Quinn were with him. Reid, who she recalled was a twin, was the darker brother and very good looking, though there was a definite conceit to him that made her grimace.

"Please don't let the rest of the princes be like him," she whispered under her breath, as she looked at the handsome

Quinn. The Var men were nothing like she'd pictured the night before. They were strong, handsome, and too charming for their own good. When doing the physical exams on the guards, she'd turned down more marriage proposals than she'd ever imagined getting in five lifetimes, let alone one day. Surely, they'd been joking, but it'd done wonders for her ego as a woman.

"Dr. Elliot?" a nearby technician asked. He was in the middle of signing a clipboard when he'd heard Tori speak.

Tori cleared her throat, "Nothing. Carry on."

Tori did her best to look dignified, as she went to stand before the head table. The king looked stressed, not that she could blame him. Having your kingdom beset by foreign scientists and HIA personnel couldn't make for an easy time. Tori stopped and waited until she gained the king's attention. When he turned to look at her, she bowed her head in respect.

"The palace is clear, your highness," she stated clearly. A couple of the scientists stopped to look curiously at her. She motioned at them to carry on. Tori paused, waiting for them to roll the heavy cart of equipment past before turning forward once more. The last thing she wanted was an audience right now. Her nerves were shot and she needed every last bit of her energy to make sure she didn't give Prince Quinn an opening to embarrass her. "My scientists have done a final sweep of the grounds and are loading the equipment back onto our ship."

"Thank you, doctor," Kirill answered. He nodded down at her from the main hall table. Prince Falke approached. The commander took a seat next to his brothers. Tori shivered. He really was the most frightening of the princes--large, militant, and emotionless. She found she couldn't look him directly in the eyes. She took a hesitant step forward and lowered her voice. "Your highness, I request permission to stay on your land. I'd like to explore the caves where the crate was found and run some tests."

"Has there been a leak?" Kirill asked alarmed. His long black hair flowed over his shoulders, nearly matching the color of his brown-black eyes. He gazed down at her, concerned.

Tori shook her head in denial. "No, but it never hurts to be careful."

"Dr. Elliot found a piece of mud caked to the crate and analyzed it. She believes there is something strange about our marshes. She wishes to run some tests," Quinn put forth.

Tori had expected him to speak, yet she wasn't prepared for it. Her heart fluttered nervously. She couldn't stop herself from glancing in his direction. Quinn's handsome face lit up with mischief and he winked at her, blowing her a gentle kiss with his lips. She knew he only teased her, but it worked for she lost her train of thought. Hardening herself, she swallowed nervously and prayed no one saw how he disturbed her.

"All that, naturally, would be in my report, your highness. The HIA will also do a planetary scan. It's just a precaution and only with your permission, of course. I'll set up camp with a team of three. You won't be bothered by us. We're scientists and won't cause any trouble. We wish to analyze the cave to make sure we've gotten all biological weaponry off the planet that might be missed with a scan. Surely you can see the wisdom in that. At the same time, I'd like to do a concise analysis of the land. If anything, my findings might actually benefit you and your people, making for more viable farmland."

"What does your Agency say?" Kirill asked.

"I don't work for the Agency. I was contracted for this one job. Their people couldn't make it here in time." Tori paused, refusing to look at Quinn though she could feel his eyes on her. "However, if you would rather have government hacks traipsing about your kingdom...." Tori shrugged.

"Write you proposal, doctor," Kirill answered, suppressing a grin, but not before she saw it. "Give it to my brother, Prince Quinn. He'll give it his approval and oversee the project."

"But, your highness!" she began, before she could stop the words. She glanced at Quinn. He wasn't smiling, but the mischief was still in his bright blue gaze. She shivered, wondering how such an aggravating man could have such a profound effect on her. It had to be sleep deprivation. There was no other reasoning for it. Slowly, she nodded, "Thank you."

Quinn watched the beautiful scientist walk away, suppressing his grin. He knew he aggravated her, but he couldn't seem to help himself. There was something about her that made him want, no *need*, to tease her. When he saw her serious face, he just felt ... playful.

When they were alone, Kirill said to Quinn, "Approve her plan if you can. We need to have those caves checked out and she's the only expert I know of on this planet. Besides, she has an honest face. I think we can trust her."

Quinn nodded. He was secretly glad someone would be checking out the caves to make sure they were safe. And if the little doctor wanted to play in the mud while she was at it, then he'd just have to make sure he was around to play with her.

* * * *

Tori sighed, staring around the metal cabin of the ESC ship. Lifting her pack over her shoulder, she turned to go. After speaking to Franklin, the Var agreed to let her and her team stay without her written proposal. It seemed when the HIA wanted something, they got it. It was just as well. She hated bureaucratic paperwork. Not too many of the ESC scientists were willing to set up camp on the Qurilixen surface with her. Most of them were contracted and couldn't leave the corporation anyway, even if they had wanted to.

Dr. Simon Martens, an older gentleman, agreed because of his passionate interest in documenting alien insect species. Simon was a round, balding figure who squinted when he talked and often got distracted from his purpose. However, he had a long solid reputation that would come in handy when it came time to add legitimacy to any project she might wish to fund.

Dr. Grant and Dr. Vitto were both younger scientists, not as experienced but both likeable enough characters. She'd worked with them both on their last assignments, and many others, so she wasn't worried. Dr. Grant was blond and tanned, even after spending months away from the sun below the icy surface of Sintaz. Dr. Vitto had short dark brown hair and bold features that bespoke of his old European earth heritage.

Part of her wanted to kick herself for taking on another project, changing her plans of a much deserved trip of relaxation to spend who knew how many months on a savage planet collecting mud samples for analysis. She'd camped before and she could easily do it again.

Tori thought of Prince Quinn. He was only too happy to give his approval to her project. She had a feeling she would be seeing a lot more of the prince. Sighing, Tori made her way down the long corridor. She knew the only thing that made the assignment bearable was that she wouldn't be at the palace during her stay.

Chapter Three

"Dr. Elliot, this will be your room for the duration of your stay."

Tori frowned at the Var guard before stepping into the luxurious palace suite after him. The pack fell from her shoulder to land on the tile floor with a loud thud. She left it where it was, stepping forward to look around.

Her jaw dropped, as she looked up toward the ceiling. A large crystal chandelier hung beneath a dome of tinted glass. It would take five men, arms spread wide, just to make a ring around the fixture. The crystal shards hung down like raindrops, lighting the large oval room.

The guard made his way around to the side wall. Tori closed her mouth and followed him with her tired eyes. The suite was just amazing.

"Food simulator," he stated, showing her where the button was hidden on the wall next to a long banner with the Var royal symbol of an upright wild cat. "I'm also to extend an invitation to you from the king that you may join the palace in the banquet hall for meals while you're here, if you prefer. Many in the palace choose to gather in the hall."

The guard, who made for an odd tour guide, looked at her expectantly. Tori nodded that she understood the invitation. A small smile lit his face, shining in the depths of his eyes. It was the same look all the Var guards had been giving her since her arrival. It was a look of open invitation.

"Over here," the guard continued, moving to where a purple velvet curtain hung from the ceiling. He stepped up on the platform and drew the curtain back. "You will find a bath."

Tori saw a large round tub surrounded by curtained windows. The velvet drapes could be drawn back for light or around the front and over the windows for privacy.

"The ceiling light will keep it dimly lit within the curtains, if you wish to have them drawn."

She again nodded at the guard. His eyes roamed down over her body and his expression glazed. Clearing her throat to get his attention off her breasts, she shot him an expectant look. The last thing she needed was this man picturing her in the bath. She was tired and just wanted to crash onto the nearest bed. She wanted darkness and a pillow. That was all. It was almost midnight and the sunlight had only dwindled to a soft haze. She again glanced up at the ceiling.

"The fireplace is lit by command," the man said, passing by the large circular fireplace across from the front door. It was designed to heat the whole room at once--bath, couches in front of it, or the side opposite the bath, which she guessed was a bed hidden by more purple curtains. The guard stopped and, gesturing to the last set of curtains, confirmed her suspicion. "This is the bed. If you wish for darkness, all you have to do is draw the curtains around as they are now."

Tori again nodded. The man smiled at her, not moving from the room.

"Navid, was it?" she asked.

"Yes," the guard grinned, gazing at her oddly.

"Thank you, Navid, for the tour." Tori gave him an awkward smile.

"Hmm, yes ... oh, yes," he said. "Very good. If you have need of anything at all, just ask Siren."

Navid made his way to the door. Tori moved to follow him, watching him bow as she closed the door behind him. She moved to step back, stopped, and then locked the door for good measure.

Without bothering to pick up her bag from the floor, she kicked off her shoes and walked toward the curtained bed. Her lab coat slipped from her arms and floated to the floor behind her. She didn't bother to take off the black jumpsuit. This wouldn't be the first time she slept in it. Struggling with the heavy purple velvet, she finally found an opening. Her eyes closed before she ever hit the soft thick mattress. Large silk pillows surrounded her and a moan escaped her lips as she relaxed against them.

"Mm, finally. I thought you'd never get here."

Tori's eyes popped open in surprise. She held perfectly still, not daring to believe her ears. A hand came from the darkness to skim across her stomach, shooting warm fire through her body, making her tingle with liquid awareness. She swatted the fingers back and they stopped with little protest. Sitting up on the bed, she belatedly screamed and reached for the curtains.

Tori stumbled from the dark bed back to the floor. Turning, huffing in anger, she glared at Prince Quinn. At least, she convinced herself it was anger that made her heart pound and her blood boil. The alternative was too unacceptable.

"What are you doing here?" she demanded, hands on hips.

"What?" the roguish prince shrugged. He grinned, sitting up on his elbows to lounge on the bed. His light brown hair was tousled erotically about his shoulders. His blue eyes beckoned her back to his side. She glanced at his strong hands, her stomach tingling where he'd dared to touch her. Every nerve inside her hummed with life, begging her to let him have his way. His tone was a low, seductive rumble in his chest. "You aren't happy to see me, Dr. Elliot?"

His easy tone infuriated her, more so since she found him incredibly sexy sitting atop the large sea of purple and gold silk. A sexy smile curled playfully on his lips, confident and sure. His chest was bare--toned and oh so defined. A primal urge rose inside her to jump on top of him. Her body pulsed to life. His grin widened.

"What--why would I be happy to see you?" Tori's eyes widened in disbelief. Happy wasn't exactly the word for what she was feeling at the moment. Her eyes again roamed down his long frame, hesitating at the obvious arousal between his thighs. It took everything in her to keep from panting like a fool and licking her lips.

"Well, earlier, in the hallway--" he began, with a light, meaningful gesture.

"Earlier, what?" Tori broke in. "Did you hear me say, hey, Prince, come to my room later tonight? Meet me in the bed so we can get it on? I don't think so, buddy."

Quinn laughed, an aggravatingly rich sound to her ears. She shivered again, her mouth dry. Sitting up, he gave a light shrug. "Well, not exactly with words, Dr. Elliot. It was more in the way you looked at me, stared really. In the way your body came to life with fragrant desire."

Tori's mouth opened, but nothing came out. For the life of her, she couldn't think of a single thing to say to that.

The prince's handsome features contorted into a pout, as he rose to his knees before her. "Come, Dr. Elliot, I didn't get my physical. I need you to examine me to see if I've been contaminated."

Tori's body lurched. Rampant desire filled her, rushing in her blood to heat every corner of her body. Her stomach and thighs tightened in anticipation. She swallowed, fighting her body's reaction to him. It would be so easy to jump on the bed and play his little game. Correction. It would be so *fun* to play his little game.

"Ah, yes, that's the smell I remember." The prince took a deep breath, making a great show of sniffing the air before he motioned to the bed. "What do you say, doctor? How about a little fun? Want to run those hands over my tight body and examine your patient? You look tense. Come, I'll massage you instead. I'll play doctor and you can be the patient."

His smile was altogether too lecherous. The tip of his tongue edged over the side of his full bottom lip. Her body lurched again, and again he seemed to smell her.

Yes! Oh, yes! Her mind screamed. Tori's face turned red in mortification. She pointed to the door. "Get out!"

"But--"

"No, I don't want to hear it. Get out. Where I come from, this is simply not acceptable behavior." Tori jerked her finger at the door once more and tapped her foot in annoyance--truthfully more annoyed by her reaction to him than by him. "In my culture if you want to get to know someone better, you ask them out on a proper date. You take them someplace nice--dinner, music, picnics, and plays--nice places to do nice, civilized things. You don't just show up in their bed uninvited!"

"Mm, *briallen*, is this place not nice?" Quinn's voice neared an agonizingly mischievous pout. He came before her, taking a bold step as he lifted his hand to brush over her neck. "And, believe me, what I have in mind to do will be a very *nice* thing to do. I promise that you'll enjoy yourself so much that you'll be screaming out my name for more."

His touch was warm, his eyes just as much so. Heat, pure and intense, washed over her from his glancing fingers. Her lips parted for breath. She couldn't move, couldn't speak, as he held her transfixed with his bright blue eyes. He was really a handsome man with a kind, laughing face. His features weren't too hard and defined--not like his brothers, but neither were they too soft. His body, on the other hand, was defined, toned, and gorgeous. It moved with relaxed grace and she could easily see him lounging before a fire, as warm and comfortable to snuggle into as a thick blanket.

"Let me pleasure you, Dr. Elliot. Say yes to me. Let me make love to you right here on this bed." His mouth drew closer. "Or the bath, the floor, the couch, wherever and however you wish it."

"No," she whispered, weak. His mouth hovered close to hers for a moment. Her eyes began to drift closed, waiting in anticipation for that contact.

"Oh, very well, Dr. Elliot." Quinn moved his hand away and stepped back. She didn't close her eyes, as she stood before him, panting for breath. A heavy sigh left him. "Get some rest. I'll see you tomorrow. We can discuss this more then."

A small sound of strangled disappointment came from the back of her throat. Her lips moved in protest, but he was already turned around and walking toward the door. She couldn't help it as her eyes dipped over the strong line of his spine to his hard butt. This man was just too much.

"There's nothing to discuss, your ... *prince-liness*," she shot after a long pause--too long a pause.

"Good night, Doctor. Sweet dreams and may they be of me--naked and thrusting above you." Quinn's fingers lifted to wave at her and he chuckled softly. Without a backward glance, he left her alone.

"Oh my," Tori said softly, feeling as if her body was on fire. She was almost too afraid to move so she stood frozen to her spot. His touch had done something to her, something that made her body tighten and throb in all the right places. Her breasts tingled and ached. The muscles of her sex clenched together. One brush of his fingers and she was brought close to orgasming. Breathless, she panted, "Oh, my. What in the world was that?"

Tori slowly crawled onto the bed. The silk felt good on her skin and before she stopped to think, she'd stripped down naked on top of it. Her fingers roamed over her body, tweaking and pinching her overly responsive length. Closing her eyes, she thought of Quinn. His sexy blue gaze danced before her, and she couldn't help but conjure the image of his tight body above hers, thrusting inside her, as she tweaked her fingers over her nipples. She held onto the image of him, reaching between her thighs to stroke her tender flesh.

With little help from her fingers, she came to climax against her hand. Her head turned and she bit the pillow next to her to keep from crying out. Even though she'd met release, she felt empty deep inside and wanting of more-- much more. When the tremors subsided and her body lay temporarily sated, all she could think to whisper was, "Oh, my."

* * * *

"Excuse me, what do you mean they canceled our trip into the forest?" Tori placed her hands on her hip and looked at the guard. This day wasn't going as planned. "Has something happened? The king told us we could leave today. We are ready to leave today. I don't understand. If there has been an accident, I need to get out there to contain it."

Tori frowned at the guard. She'd spent only one night in the palace and the whole of the morning packing her supplies, doing her best not to run into Prince Quinn before she left. She didn't wish to "discuss" anything with him. That man was more complication than any woman needed-- especially a woman like her who had more than two brain cells in her head.

To her shame, she dreamt of the prince the night before and it hadn't been completely innocent. Okay, there was nothing innocent about what they'd been doing in her mind--or in what positions they'd been doing them in. Tori swallowed down the blush the memory brought to her cheeks. She was never, ever, *ever* telling a soul about that one. Some things were better left taken to the grave.

"I've got all of my supplies readied," she said needlessly, motioning to the crates behind her.

"There's no accident," the guard said in a low tone. He smiled at her, causing her frown to deepen. Every time one of the Var men looked at her, she felt like a piece of meat about to be pounced upon. "Today is a day of celebration, not work. No one will be traveling from the palace until tomorrow, perhaps the next day if the celebration is done right. A guard cannot be spared to guide you."

"What celebration?" Tori asked.

"I heard the king is getting married," Simon offered at her side.

Dr. Grant and Dr. Vitto came up behind the older scientist. They didn't look ready to go. It was clear someone had already told them of the change of plans. Tori bit her lip in irritation. *She* was in charge, not these bozos! She would definitely be having a talk with someone to point that little fact out. Shivering, she realized that someone was probably Quinn.

"Yeah, all guests are expected to attend the feast." Grant rubbed his hands together, throwing out a careless, pretty boy smile at her. It's how he looked at everyone, so she ignored it. Turning to Vitto, he chuckled, "I heard they have a harem full of beautiful women who'll be attending."

Vitto grinned, but said nothing. Tori turned to glare at him.

"What?" Vitto demanded, lifting his hands up like a scolded kid. His lip jutting out in a pout, he asked, "What did I do? Grant said it."

"Hey," Grant pushed Vitto in the side. Then shrugging, he laughed, "It's true though. They do have a harem. They said the women are lonely since the old king died and are looking for ... er ... manly comfort."

Vitto laughed. Even Simon's ears seemed to perk up.

Tori sighed. Under her breath, she muttered to the ceiling, "They've sent me children. I asked for scientists and they gave me children."

"Hey, we're all adults," Grant said, knowing Tori only teased them. They'd spent a lot of time together and felt more like siblings than colleagues. "Listen, I've been frozen in an ice block for only God remembers how many months with only you guys." Tori lifted a brow and he quickly added, "Sorry, Elliot, but you don't count 'cause you turned me down. Now, I'm counting you as a guy because of it. Unless of course you'd like to reconsider my very tempting offer?"

Tori made a gagging motion at him and he shrugged. Vitto slugged him lightly in the shoulder.

"Your loss, babycakes," Grant answered, unhampered.

"I know you didn't just call me babycakes," Tori grimaced, trying to hide her laughter.

"What? Me? No, sweetcheeks, I'd never be so disrespectful. You're lead scientist on this expedition and we all know that order must be maintained at all times, right, love button?" Grant grinned. Her mouth opened and he hurried before she could interject. "We've been working really hard and we all deserve a little S and M, Dr. Elliot, sir, ma'am. I know I could use some."

"Don't you mean R and R?" Vitto asked, chuckling.

"Oh, yeah," Grant laughed good-naturedly and shrugged. "That's the one. So easy to get them confused. But, I'm sure Elliot here knows all about that, don't ya, Elliot?"

"R and R?"

Tori froze. Prince Quinn would have to show himself at that moment. She glanced around, wondering if she could duck out gracefully before he saw her. Too late. His eyes were directly on her face. She colored slightly.

"Prince Quinn," Tori acknowledge politely, professionally, when he didn't look away from her.

"Dr. Elliot," Quinn returned, not so professional.

A strange silence came over the group as he stared. Her mind chose that moment to recall the vividness of her dreams and the details of his naked chest as he knelt playfully on her bed. Her cheeks tried to flame with embarrassment, but she swallowed it down, doing her best to remain professional and calm. Her heart sped in her chest, racing to be free. What was it about this man that sent her senses over the edge? She cleared her throat uncomfortably. Vitto stepped next to her, standing a little too close.

"R and R. Rest and relaxation," Vitto offered with a smile. "It's what we say when we need a much deserved break from work."

"Ah, and S and M?" Quinn inquired, glancing back to Tori.

"Sleep and m..." Tori faltered. She couldn't think of anything. She looked desperately to Grant, but he just shrugged and offered no help. "Ma-massages."

Quinn's mouth opened. Vitto shot his hand forward in offering.

"Hi, I don't believe we've met. Everyone calls me Vitto. This is Dr. Grant, ignore anything he says--none of it is true. We're not actually sure he's a real doctor, but we let him come along anyway. And this distinguished gentleman is Dr. Simon Marten."

Quinn nodded politely at them all, grinning at the lively introduction. "So, did I hear you gentlemen speaking of our harem?"

Tori paled, mildly disgusted. She rolled her eyes. Worse than the harem was the fact that the prince had heard their entire conversation. She was sure she was going to be sick--right after she killed Grant.

Grant cleared his throat, "Yeah, I'm sorry--"

"Think nothing of it," Quinn chuckled pleasantly. "The women are free to do as they wish. We don't own them. Actually, I believe my brother wishes for them to find husbands, so please, feel free to take them off his hands."

"Your brother the king?" Grant asked. "The one whose wedding is tonight."

"Actually, his ... ah, wedding, as you call it, was technically yesterday. I believe they mated themselves on the side balcony."

"You believe?" Tori asked, frowning. Mated? Did everyone just drop their pants and *mate* anywhere they pleased?

Quinn saw her look and laughed. "Mated as in got married, Dr. Elliot."

Tori gasped lightly. Then, since her mouth was already open, she asked, "You don't know where your brother was married?"

"You will find our culture isn't so longwinded when it comes to ceremony. Once a decision is made, there is no reason to wait or put it off for later. Marriage only takes two people who wish it. They say it, it is done. Simple. Tonight is the queen's coronation banquet. The king and queen will also be officially announcing the queen's pregnancy. We'd love it if you'd all join us in celebrating our family's good fortune."

"We'd be honored," Simon answered for them, patting down his gray hair.

Grant shot a meaningful look at Vitto and wiggled his eyebrows. Tori looked at them and sighed. The guys had been working as hard as she and they all deserved a break. Vitto turned to her with the "please, please, please" look begging in his eyes. Slowly, Tori nodded.

"We'd be honored," Tori mimicked, forcing a smile.

"Wonderful!" Quinn exclaimed. "Now, if you would, come to the hall and dine with us. We'd love to have you--"

"No, thank you," Tori interjected, grabbing an electronic clipboard from the top of the crate. All eyes turned to her as she inched away. "You guys go ahead. If we're not leaving, I have some details to work out and a report to start."

Tori turned to walk down the hall.

"Ah, Dr. Elliot," Quinn said. "One moment, please."

Tori stopped and closed her eyes. She took a deep breath and slowly turned on her heels to face the men.

"It would be my honor to escort you tonight to the celebration," Prince Quinn said, unashamed that every man around them heard his offer. Tori's cheeks stained slightly.

"No, I don't think that will be necessary. I'm sure I can find my way to the hall just fine. Thank you," she quipped.

"Actually, Dr. Elliot, this would be a date," Prince Quinn stated, smiling. Mischief sparkled in his eyes. "You know, going someplace nice to do nice things. I believe "date" is the word of your earth custom."

"Oh, yeah," Grant offered, not at all helpful. "That's the one all right."

Tori froze, mortified. Vitto and Grant stared at each other then at Tori with wide-eyed wonder. Or was it wide-eyed mocking? Tori's mouth opened, then closed, opened again. The Var prince was asking her out on a date. How in the galaxy was she going to say no without risking his anger? And what in the galaxy was he going to expect to happen on this date? A weak sound left her throat as she began to shake her head. Looking desperately to Vitto, she said, "Thank you, but I think Dr. Vitto will be escorting me tonight."

"Not this time," Vitto said, grinning from ear to ear and making an insolent face to her behind the prince's back. Smirking, he said, "I already have a date. Grant's asked me."

Vitto nudged Grant and grinned wider so Prince Quinn couldn't see. Grant winked back at him. Tori grimaced, turning her pleading gaze to Grant for help. She should've known better. He gave her a wicked grin, blew her a kiss, and slowly shook his head in denial. Almost frantically, she leaned over to find Simon. His back was turned to them, as he pretended to examine a crate. Tori bit her lip and swallowed a curse. All three of them were going to be in so much trouble when she got a hold of them later. When she was through with them, they'd be on permanent food rations and three hour sleep shifts.

Quinn's bright blue gaze hadn't moved from her face. She looked directly at him, feeling at a loss for words. The smile faded from his teasing lips, but the amusement remained in his eyes.

No one spoke. Vitto motioned frantically at her to answer. Slowly, she nodded, "Very well, I would lov--*like* very much to be escorted by you."

Grant and Vitto tried to hide their laughter and failed miserably. They snickered like two children. She shot them a glare of warning. Simon merely grinned at the younger doctors' antics, staying out of it as he looked up from his crate.

"Wonderful!" Quinn exclaimed, smiling once more.

Tori's brows rose on her forehead. She weakly nodded and turned back around. With quick steps, she hurried away before they could stop her again. As she took the corner, a round of masculine laughter burst from the group.

Quinn turned to look at the two laughing scientists and chuckled. "I guess I should thank you for helping me out."

"If you're going after Elliot, you need all the help you can get," Grant said, sniffing back tears of merriment.

"Yeah, don't thank us yet," Vitto put forth. "She's a handful."

"Ah, man, do you remember Schreoder?" Grant shook his head mournfully. "He tried to ask her out on a date for like a month--"

"Oh, yeah, I think that poor man is still tying to recover his manhood," Vitto interjected. He glanced slyly at Quinn who didn't seem to notice, as the prince's eyes were looking toward where Tori disappeared. "Man, just make sure you don't talk about anything she might take offense to. Last scientist that she dated said he thought the ADP complex was a hoax. She publicly hung him out to dry."

Quinn listened to the two men, wondering at the jealousy he suddenly felt at their words. It was apparent they knew Dr. Elliot fairly well. Vitto had stood protectively close to her. He couldn't help but wonder how well they knew her. Come to think of it, he didn't even know her first name.

"The key to Elliot is not to treat her too much like a lady. She likes to hold her own." Grant looked to Vitto for confirmation.

"Oh, yeah, definitely." Vitto nodded. "She hates it when men take her arm, open doors, pull out chairs. It drives her crazy. She's a real feminist."

"Well, thank you for the advice," Quinn answered. He began to step away, before turning. "By the way, the ADP complex was a hoax. The man was faking the disorder."

As Quinn walked away, Vitto and Grant's jaws dropped. It was true. It had been a hoax, but both scientists were amazed the prince had even heard of it. When they were alone, both men began to chuckle.

"Oh man, she is going to eat him alive," Grant snickered. "When you called her a feminist I almost wet myself. It was too funny. Our Elliot, a feminist!"

Chapter Four

Tori took a deep breath, trying to calm her nerves. Her heart raced erratically in her chest, thudding so loud she was sure it echoed outside her body. She looked at her reflection in the full size mirror and sighed. It had been a long time since she put on anything that wasn't a lab coat and jumpsuit. She'd been surprised when the guard handed her the box from Prince Quinn with the instructions he would be by to pick her up that evening.

The gown she wore looked much like the Var style of dress. It had a soft, glimmering black material that glistened with silver when she moved. It draped beautifully, hugging her breasts and hips. The neckline scooped down, baring a fair amount of cleavage. She blushed to think Quinn picked it out for that feature alone.

Cross laces worked along her sides, exposing the flesh of her waist and hips. She'd tried to wear underwear with it, but she couldn't keep the sides of her panties from showing through, so finally she took them off. She was a little uncomfortable being so exposed. The dress had built in support so a bra wasn't necessary.

After taking a water bath, which Tori thoroughly enjoyed, she carefully covered herself in lotion and perfume. Spending a lot of time on remote planets, she had taken a number of water baths in her lifetime and found them to be one of the ultimate pleasures.

Hair styling was another matter altogether, but she managed to pin up the sides with what little she had to work with. The heavy brown locks dried with natural waves and she let them flow down over her shoulders instead of pulling it back into a serviceable bun. With a nod, she decided she was very pleased with her appearance.

Hearing a knock on the door, she stiffened. That had to be Quinn. Her fingers shook as she moved across the suite to answer it. When she pulled the door open, she stiffened. It was Quinn and he looked absolutely gorgeous. Her heart did little fluttering somersaults in her chest, making her instantly lightheaded. His light brown hair flowed down over his shoulders, framing his face to perfection. His bright blue eyes bore playfully into her and she realized he just couldn't seem to help himself. He always looked like he was up to something mischievous.

Tori began to open her mouth, but he held up a finger to silence her. Slowly, he let his eyes roam over her body, scorching her with the fire of his perusal. She couldn't help but do the same to him. He wore the traditional clothes of his people, crossed laced shirts and pants that exposed the sides and hips. Leather boots molded over his calves. Damned, but he was too sexy for his own good and, by the smirk on his face, he knew it.

She waited breathlessly for him to say something romantic. His eyes moved back up her, as potent as a caress. His mouth opened to speak. A slow smile tried to creep onto her features.

"That dress looks hot on you," Quinn stated, grinning. "But it'd look better off of you and crumpled on the bedroom floor."

Her smile fell. Quinn boldly laughed as he stepped in. Waving his hand behind him, he motioned a group of guards forward. Their arms were laden with gifts, which they promptly set around the suite. Tori stood before him speechless.

"I looked up your earth dating customs, since you're insistent you want me to bring you on a date before you let me into your bed." When her mouth opened to deny him, he rushed on. She wasn't sure what she'd say with the guards there anyway. "No, don't worry. I have no problem playing it your way. There was quite a bit of information, but I managed to secure all the necessary items."

Tori made a weak, baffled sound as she tried to shake her head. The guards left just as quickly as they entered. Quinn shut the door behind them. When he turned back to her, he winked.

Tori watched, speechless, as the prince crossed over to a giant block of chocolate sitting on a large silver platter. The hunk was twice the size of his head and had taken two guards to carry. "Lithorian chocolate, the best in the galaxy."

"Quinn--"

"Wait, I'm not done." He motioned to a strange bird that looked like a stuffed earth turkey, only with razor sharp teeth and claws. The hideous thing was mounted on a wooden plank. "We didn't have a stuffed bear. And, since I'm not even sure what sort of beast a teddy bear is or where one would find it, I brought you a stuffed baldric instead. It will have to suffice."

"Quinn, I--"

"Wait, there's more." He gave her an exasperated sigh at her interruption and motioned at about five vases overflowing with a pale white flower with blue centers and brown stems. "These are solarflowers, native but rare to this planet. Again, didn't have roses, so these will have to be sufficient."

Tori didn't even bother to speak this time when he paused. She kept her mouth closed, watching him, completely baffled.

"According to your royal king and queen tradition of..." Quinn stopped, thought a minute, and said, "...high school prom. You're supposed to wear a gown and I'm supposed to give you a shower."

"A shower?" Tori asked, confused. Her eyes narrowed in suspicion.

"Yes, a corsage, which when I looked it up, meant spray. When I looked up spray it meant shower. You already have the gown. So, if you come with me, I will happily put a shower on you." Quinn stepped toward her. An excited gleam entered his eyes as he tried to reach for her.

Tori shook her head and backed up. "Uh, I already had a bath, thank you. And I believe the word corsage is also just a flower you pin onto your chest or wrist."

"Earth men pin flowers into their women? Doesn't it hurt?" He looked horrified. "Do you find there is a problem with blood loss due to artery--?"

"No, to the clothes," Tori quickly amended. Weakly, she said, "They pin the flowers to the clothes."

"Ah," Quinn sighed. "That makes more sense. You earth women have a thing for flowers then. I always thought they were more like weeds, but the harem women seem fond enough of them too. Very well, I will have more vases delivered before we get back tonight and I will pin them all over your dress."

"What's the pitcher for?" Tori asked, almost afraid of the answer as she changed the subject. Stuffed turkeys, a mountain of chocolate, showers--she didn't know how many more earth customs she could take.

"It is wine. We don't bottle our liquor and I thought this was better than a barrel. Though, if you wish for the barrel, I can have one brought to you--"

"No, no, the pitcher is perfect." Tori forced a polite smile, though what she really wanted to do was laugh. When she thought about it, though all wrong, it really was sweet of him to make the effort--even if he was doing it just to get into her panties.

"Great!" Quinn grinned. "So, let's go to this coronation and then we can come back here and have sex."

"Wait, just because you do all this, doesn't mean we're going to have sex," Tori stated, her cheeks flushed. Did this man never give up?

"Yes, I was afraid of that." Quinn nodded and then winked. "But, you can't blame a man for trying. Every time I'm around you, I smell your longing and it clouds my judgment. I know it will be soon. I can wait for you to know it as well."

"Oh, um," Tori sighed and gave him a helpless smile. "It's not poetry, but it's ... not even close to poetry actually."

The playful look he shot her was utterly stunning in its simplicity. Holding out his arm, he asked, "Shall we go, my lady?"

* * * *

The banquet hall was filled with the Var people who'd come to see their new queen. Tori was a little unsettled to be at the head table next to Quinn and the royal family, where all the attention was being directed. She saw many speculative glances cast her way and she couldn't help but wonder what they were thinking.

Several times during the long meal, Quinn's fingers would stray to her thigh and twice he got so bold as to dip his hand behind her back and into the cross laces of her gown. His warm fingers on her flesh nearly wrenched a scream from her lips, as a shockwave of pleasure assaulted her. When she didn't hit him right away, a grin spread over his features and Tori was forced to wiggle away from his touch.

"So," Tori began, looking at Quinn as the plates were taken away. Traditional Var music played in the background. It was beautiful, but she missed her oldie earth tunes. She was on the end of the head table, away from Quinn's brothers so she had no one else to talk to. "Tell me more about the houses of Var and Draig."

"The Draig have been the enemy of the Var since before I was born. My father believed that we were too different to coexist in peace." Quinn shrugged and leaned back in his chair to study her. "But now Kirill is working for peace."

"You don't want peace?" Tori asked.

"I want what is best for the Var people."

When he spoke of his duty and his people, she saw a rare seriousness in his eyes that wasn't there at other times. Quinn may be playful, but he was also very dedicated to his job and his position in Var society. His love for his culture and his race ran deep.

During dinner, Quinn spoke of his people and their great history--a history the princes had lived through. The Var lived a long time and sometimes passed that long life on to their life mates--aided by the same mystical power that guided them and the radiation from the blue sun.

He told her much about the former King Attor's rule. From what she already knew about him bringing the biological weapons to his own planet, Tori was kind of glad he was dead. She would hate to have met him. It was an opinion she wisely kept to herself.

Long ago, several hundred years before the princes' birth, before Attor became king, things had been different for the Var people. It was a wild time, a time when the Var let emotions rule their heads and their hearts. They acted rashly and on pure instinct. Looking at the charming Quinn and his never-ending barrage of come-on lines, she doubted very much that things had changed as much as he'd have her believe.

For reasons completely unknown to his son, Attor changed the ways of the Var. He was a good king, one who worked hard for his people. He encouraged emotional detachment so that if one halfmate died, there could be others to take her place. It was Attor who encouraged men to have control, to drink *nef*--a drink that somehow calmed them sexually and gave them restraint. When she swallowed nervously at that, Quinn grinned and said, "Don't worry. I never really liked the stuff and don't drink it."

Tori blushed profusely and quickly took a drink of her wine to hide her red face. Quinn chuckled in response and ran a hand lightly over her spine. She nearly fell off the chair with the jolt of pleasure it gave her.

King Attor had urged the Var men to prove their worth and dependability with emotionless detachment. He taught by example that to prove great prowess in the bedroom showed prowess in the field of battle, until strength in one meant strength in the other. Many of the elders followed the old king's example and took many halfmates, though none so many as the king. Life mates were a privilege of the lower classes--tradesmen, farmers, even hunters and lower ranked soldiers, all men who could ill afford to keep many mates on a planet so barren of women to begin with.

That is why the fact that King Kirill took a queen as a life mate was such a big deal. Many of the elders, especially the one called Lord Myrddin, wouldn't look favorably upon the decision. However, many of the Var people would. The rumors of Queen Ulyssa's sacrifice for them in looking for the biological weapon had been widely spread. By the glint in his eye, it was easy for Tori to see Quinn had a hand in spreading those rumors.

King Attor's father, Quinn's grandfather, had suffered the folly of mating with one woman. She died when Attor was born and his father never recovered enough to breed more women for sons. Although he took women to his bed, he left Attor without any brothers to help lead the Var nation. So, when Attor took over the throne, he became reliant on a few noble houses--like Lord Myrddin's. Even when Attor had his sons, he relied heavily upon the old house nobles. With Kirill as the new king, the old house nobles were no longer needed, for Kirill had his brothers. Lord Myrddin wasn't happy to be out of power. It was a new era for the Var.

Lord Myrddin was the technical owner of the land she'd be camping on. Since the king decreed she would go,

Quinn assured her she shouldn't have a problem with the old Var lord. Tori wasn't so confident. Angry, desperate men in power made her nervous and she didn't want to be caught in some kind of political crossfire.

"You should allow me to take this cream back with us to your suite. I would love to lick it from your body."

Tori blinked in surprise. She'd been lost in thought and nearly choked on her drink at his words. For awhile, besides the wandering hands, Quinn had been acting like a perfect gentleman--opening doors, pulling out her chair, leading her about on his arm, politely introducing her to those who came to the table to greet the new queen. He'd even referred to her as a guest of the greatest honor. Glancing down at the table, she saw the servants had left a cream covered dessert before them.

The idea of Quinn licking it off her naked breasts was almost too much. She pushed the dessert away and focused on not being aroused. She didn't want him "smelling" her reaction to his comments. It was almost unfair that he could sense when she became turned on by him. Before she could answer, a woman's voice broke into her concentration.

"Someone pulled all the solarflowers from the side lawn near the harem." Taura said, with a very dignified nod of her head. She was a tall, stately woman with long willowy limbs--very characteristic of her Roane heritage. Her gown of gold shimmered as she moved. Her long, golden brown hair fell in shiny waves down her back, the color mimicked by the hazel-gold of her almond shaped eyes. She was a beautiful woman and Tori could instantly see why Attor had chosen her as his first halfmate.

Taura was also Prince Falke's birth mother. Tori didn't see how such a slender woman could give birth to a giant like the commander prince. According to the introduction she'd been given to the woman, she'd been a mother to all the princes--especially when their own birth mothers had died. At her words, Quinn paled slightly and looked like a kid caught with his hand in the cookie jar. Tori realized that the flowers were in her room were stolen from Taura's flower garden. He had said they were rare.

"Ah, Dr. Elliott," the king stated. He leaned forward to block Quinn from Taura's view, as he saved his little brother from getting caught. He gave Quinn a knowing look, which Taura on his other side couldn't see. "Have you got all your provisions?"

Tori looked across the banquet table to the king and nodded. "Yes, thank you. The HIA has left us well taken care of."

Tori saw Queen Ulyssa smile slightly at her words. She really was beautiful with her red-blonde hair and dark blue eyes. Whenever the woman looked up at her husband, it was with utter love and devotion. Tori turned back to her meal, wondering at the sudden jealousy and longing that assaulted her senses when she saw the happy couple. She glanced at Quinn, feeling him all the way down to her toes. Her body wanted him that was for sure. But she knew it simply wasn't wise to get involved with him. He was a prince, her key to staying on the planet, and Tori knew better than to mix business and pleasure--no matter how cute the pleasure was.

On the other hand, it wasn't like either of them were attached or in danger of becoming attached. Tori shook her head, refusing to consider it. What was she thinking? He was royalty! You just didn't have a casual affair with royalty on a whim and she certainly wasn't going to justify sleeping with Quinn just because she was hot for him. No, once she got away from him and the palace, she'd be able to put it all into perspective. Until she could consider all sides and make a logical, rational decision, nothing was going to happen between her and the handsome Var prince.

* * * *

Quinn walked the lovely scientist through the long, mazelike halls of the palace as they made their way back to the guest suite. When he first saw her in the gown he gave her, it took his breath away. It pleased him that she wore it. He'd been scared her stubborn nature would've refused the gift.

There was something about Dr. Elliot that captured him. Her smell, her look, her voice--it all drove him to distraction. He wanted her desperately, but was willing to wait for her. He just prayed to all his gods that she didn't make him wait too long. Quinn was a patient, easygoing man, but even he had his limits.

Dr. Elliot did something to him, something he'd never felt before. When he touched her, he felt all hot and cold at the same time. His body stirred to her, like it had never stirred to anyone. When her gaze lingered too long on one of the guards, he grew jealous and ready to fight to win her attention back--like by dipping his hands beneath her dress to make her shiver.

Sacred Cats! She had skin like silk, warm smooth silk. Quinn suppressed a groan, feeling her on his hands even now.

It was true Dr. Elliot had burrowed beneath his skin. Maybe it was because she obviously wanted him, yet sought to deny them both. Or, maybe it was the way her hips moved beneath the glimmering black gown. Quinn's eyes became heavy and his breathing deepened. He slowed his step, as they rounded a corner, just so he could check out her firm butt again. Biting his lip to keep from moaning, he briefly closed his eyes and shook his head. Yep, it could definitely be the way her hips moved beneath the gown. It took all his willpower not to grab her up against the wall. If he never drank *nef* before, he might just have to start drinking it now. The degree to which he was aroused, he really needed to be sedated to keep it under control.

Without thought, the prince reached over, grabbed a cheek firmly in his palm, and squeezed. Tori yelped and looked over her shoulder at him. Quinn shot her an audacious grin, refusing to look at all apologetic. Why should he apologize for wanting her? It wasn't as if his attention was insulting. He kept his hand on her until she quickened her step and pulled away.

Tori watched Quinn from the corner of her eyes, waiting for him to make another move and secretly hoping he would. She had to admit, the man's boldness and persistence excited her as a woman. There was nothing sexier than confidence. But, as a professional, which she was most of the time, she knew it was bad for business. She stayed firm, giving him a properly chastising frown for the wandering hands before stepping out of his way.

"Dr. Grant seemed taken with Linzi," Quinn said, breaking the silence.

Tori glanced back at him in surprise. They'd walked in virtual silence and it seemed an odd topic to break it with. Quinn took the opportunity to catch back up to her side.

"Are you jealous?" Tori asked, doing her best to act nonchalant. She was teasing, though her heart did skip a little while waiting for the answer.

"Why would I be? She's not my woman," Quinn answered. He shrugged as if it were no big deal.

"But, you were in the hall...."

"Nothing happened. We were just fooling around," Quinn filled in when she hesitated.

"You say that as if it was no big deal."

"It's not. She is a woman, I'm a man. We have needs. We fulfill them. It really is a simple concept. Neither of us was attached, least of all to each other. Besides, Linzi and I were never together." Quinn reached over and picked up Tori's arm. He winked at her. "I've turned my sights to something better."

Tori blushed prettily. Okay, it was a strange compliment, but it still gave her a rush of pleasure to hear that she was "something better."

"I'm sure sex to you, Dr. Elliot, is a well calculated, academically fulfilling pursuit." Quinn smiled, showing he was partly teasing. "Tell me, do you make lists of why and why not you should choose someone as a lover?"

Tori didn't say a word. She did her best to keep from being mortified. She did make lists.

Quinn laughed. "So, what is the margin? The man must have two more positives than negatives? Do you have a list on me?"

"No," she stammered.

His face fell. "So I'm not even in the running?"

"No ... yes," Tori frowned, wrinkling her nose at him. He was only trying to fluster her and she knew it. "You are--"

"Great!" Quinn interrupted before she could finish her sentence. "Let me know how I come out. I might be able to help you tip the scales in my favor."

"That wasn't what I was saying," Tori put forth.

You are incorrigible, is what she'd been thinking.

Quinn's smile widened, as he changed the subject--somewhat. "What is so special about these scientists you date?"

Tori cleared her throat. The way he asked it made her think he'd been doing his research on her. How did he know she only dated scientists? The answer hit her like a freight train. It was so obvious--Grant and Vitto. Had she decided on three hour sleep shifts for the treacherous men? She was sure she'd meant two. "Well, for one thing, they recite poetry to a woman. They say nice, pretty things."

"Poetry?" Quinn repeated, almost in disgust. Tori nodded. The prince's brow furrowed in confusion. "Chocolates, barrels of wine, flowers? I don't understand this need for so much ceremony and custom. Now, the hunted offerings, this I get. You wish a man who is fierce enough to fight and kill a dreaded teddy bear. It's very wise to make him prove his strength. You wouldn't wish to be associated with a man who couldn't protect you in times of conflict."

Tori struggled to keep a straight face. Oh, yes, the fearsome teddy bear. Watch out for the button eyes! They could choke small, unattended infants with a single pull! Tori sniffed. It was hard not to laugh outright.

"In all seriousness," Quinn broke into her thoughts. They came to her suite door and stopped. When she looked at him, he seemed to be in very deep contemplation over the matter. "Why would you wish for these things? Flowery words memorized from a book? All that proves is they can't speak for themselves or are hiding something. Isn't honesty much sweeter?"

"It's nice to be courted. The pleasure is derived from the effort made," Tori said, though she could see the merit of his words. "Don't the Var believe in paying compliment and giving gifts to women?"

"Ah, we do, but when we compliment it's with our own words not those of someone else. I compliment you often and will continue to do so, but it's not with poetry for I'm not a poet. I'm an ambassador. I said I'd rather see your gown crumpled on the floor. That was a compliment for it is very true. There is more honor in speaking what is true than what is merely pleasant."

Tori wasn't sure what to say to his logic. The man did make a good point and he seemed very serious. As he spoke, she was almost afraid to smile for fear he'd take offense to it.

"As to gifts, we Var are very generous to our lovers and mates. We like to lavish gifts on them, especially when it gives them pleasure to receive them." Quinn's eyelids fell seductively over his heated gaze. "But, we don't require the gift giving. If it is not freely given, then a gift isn't a gift so much as a requirement. For what is the point if both parties are finding mutual pleasure? This is what confuses me about your earth customs. According to your old traditions, women receive these gifts but men do not. So are earth men paying for sex?"

"Mm, well," Tori didn't know how to answer that. She was the last person to give dating advice to anyone. Her dates usually were makeshift picnics on assignment in the middle of field research.

Nothing says romance like getting taken to an ice block to freeze your heinie off, she thought with a smirk.

"Well?" he prompted, when she didn't answer right away.

"I can't tell you. Most of those old traditions are no longer practiced in space, but only on earth itself." Tori shrugged. His face fell slightly and she rushed, "But it was a wonderful gesture on your part. I think it was very sweet."

He nodded. A silence stretched between them as he studied her.

"Well," Tori began awkwardly. "Thank you for a very lovely evening."

"It doesn't have to end," Quinn insisted, as she opened the door. He watched her walk inside only to stop and turn to him. He didn't expect her to sleep with him, but he couldn't help offering up the suggestion. Every time he came onto her, her body would emit the most intoxicating sexual smell. What could he say? He was addicted to it.

"Yes it does," she answered softly. Her dark eyes modestly lowered, before traveling back up to his face.

"Can I at least call upon the last tradition of a kiss at the end of the date?" Quinn asked. The doorframe was still between them. "That's one I actually agree with as a good idea."

Slowly, Tori nodded, but didn't move to join him in the hall. Quinn let a sexy grin curl the side of his mouth, before stepping toward her. He left the door open, not making any assumptions, as he came to stand before her.

Quinn slowly leaned over, letting his mouth work tenderly along hers. It was hard, but he kept the kiss chaste, not wishing to torture himself any more than he already was. His hands stayed at his sides, not moving to touch her, though he longed to do just that. It would be a long night and he didn't need the memory of her taste making it worse. Slowly, he pulled back and smiled. "Good night, Dr. Elliot."

"Good night, Prince Quinn," she murmured in response. Tori's heart thumped wildly. He smelled so good. Her blood raced with anticipation, making her limbs shake to hold him. Her body became hot, flooded with her desire for him. Every nerve she had tingled. At the brush of his lips to hers, she let loose a small feminine sigh. She felt him all the way to her toes.

Her nipples were hard and tingling. How in the galaxy were her nipples tingling from a brief kiss? How was it her whole body felt on fire, as if she was melting? It was only a kiss. She took several deep breaths. This was insane. She shouldn't even consider sleeping with him. She had to think logically. She had to get control. She had ... to get him out of those clothes.

Tori moaned. She couldn't control her arms as they shot forward. Wantonly, she thrust her stomach into his hard arousal, groaning to feel how hot and thick it was for her. Quinn blinked in surprise. Her body pressed tighter along his frame and her hands delved into his hair, tangling in the silken threads. Her nipples exploded with pleasure, sending shockwaves over her body. She pulled his mouth more fully to hers, making him stumble back with the force of her longing.

Quinn's shoulder hit the door and he swatted it out of the way on instinct, slamming it shut. Tori giggled against his mouth, the sound driving him mad. His fingers lifted to cup her full breasts. He'd wanted to touch them all night. He tested the weight of her in his palms, running to stroke his thumbs over the incredibly hard tips that he found buried in the soft material of her gown.

"Argh, Sacred Cats, woman!" Quinn growled, rubbing his hard arousal against her between their clothes. "You're too much."

Tori pushed him back into the door, trapping him to her body as she stroked down his chest. She clawed at his shirt, fighting with the laces to get it off his body. When she nearly howled in frustration, he pulled back.

"Allow me." Lifting a finger, he allowed her to watch as the tip of it shifted into a claw. Quinn reached to his side and, with a deft stroke, cut through the laces so that his shirt fell open. Then, just as quickly, he took the claw to her neckline and pulled it down, ripping the material open to free her large breasts. The material clung seductively to the sides of them, hiding her nipples from view but exposing the deep valley between. When he glanced back up, she stared at him in awe.

"You really can shift into a cat," she breathed. A slow, excited smile crept over her features, as she moved to reach for him. She began to pant as a new wave of heat rolled down her body. "What else can the big kitty do?"

Quinn let a low, predatory sound echo in the back of his throat. Tori stopped and backed away. She licked her lips, waiting in breathless anticipation for him to pounce.

"Does the big kitty want to come out and play?" she purred naughtily. Her wide eyes drifted down to his obvious erection.

Quinn continued to stalk her, lowering his jaw as he allowed his eyes to shift with pale green for her, letting a flash of his cat eyes bend his pupils. Instantly, he was rewarded with a hefty wafting of her feminine scent. She was more than ready for him and it drove him nearly insane to realize it. Even more arousing was the fact she accepted his Var side without fear.

Tori's legs hit the back of the couch before the fireplace. Spinning around, she thrust her butt into the air. It was more than Quinn could handle. He rushed to her, lifting her dress to bare her thighs. His fingers ran over her skin, warming her, caressing her, discovering her.

When the gown stopped his exploration, he grimaced and took a claw to the material along her back, ripping it apart. Once he had her bare, he began kissing and stroking her from behind. Despite his urgency, he took his time as he learned the workings of her body.

Tori didn't move from the couch as she threw her head back in pleasure. Her fingers gripped into the soft cushion, nearly puncturing it as he touched her. A weak sound left her throat and she wiggled her hips for attention. His fingers teased, skimming everywhere but the center heat. Fire burned a hot trail over her flesh, raging through her blood until every corner of her being sizzled with longing.

"Quinn, please," she begged, moving to stand. He pushed her back down. His fingers finally dipped between her thighs, causing her to cry out. Stroking along her soaked opening, he teased the sensitive bud he found buried in her silken folds. Then, easing a finger inside, he tested her depths, stroking firmly in a slow rhythm as she thrust herself onto his hand. She was hot, ready, nearly screaming with the agony of need.

Quinn moved his body behind her, letting her feel that he'd stripped off his clothes. The heavy length of his erection pressed into her tender skin as his hands wrapped around to grab her sensitive breasts in his palms. She was a passionate woman, more so than he'd ever imagined. Her responses were pure, natural, and primitive. She was confident in her body's reaction to him and it spurred him into a mindless web of wonder.

Edging next to her, he lightly stroked his shaft along her opening, letting her get used to the feel. To his surprise, her hips bucked back, forcing him to dip inside the rim of her body. That one feel was more than he could take. He pushed forward, burying himself to the hilt. Her muscles stretched around him, clamping down so hard he nearly lost himself.

"Ah," Tori cried out. Her fingers worked the couch. "Oh, Quinn, oh, yes, baby, yes."

Her hips moved, as she tried to get him to thrust. He instantly obeyed, drawing his hips back and forth as he moved within her. A tension built in her thighs, warming its way into her blood until she was screaming for release. At her cries, he only moved faster until he had her hips in his hands and was pounding so hard the slapping of their bodies echoed around them.

Quinn grunted. Tori screamed. Their hips rocked faster and harder, seeking the release they both desperately needed.

The tension built, nearly tearing Tori apart as she sought to end it. Then, suddenly, with a high-pitched yell, she began to tremble. Her body felt as if it fell off a cliff. Her limbs weakened and her muscles clamped tightly around him.

Quinn's soft shout of pleasure followed hers. He stiffened behind her and his body released heavily into her, milked by the clenching and unclenching of her feminine muscles. They held frozen, unable to move for a long time. Then, falling against her back, he sighed and began to caress her gently.

Tori stood, turning to wrap her arms around his neck. A small sound of contentment hummed past her lips. Quinn swooped down, capturing her lips as he kissed her breath away. Then pulling back, he grinned wickedly.

"What is your first name Dr. Elliot? I've been listening for it all night."

Tori laughed. A low growl sounded from him, making her knees weak and her heart palpitate. "Tori. It's Tori."

"Well, Tori," Quinn said, leaning forward to lick playfully at her mouth. He swept her up into his strong arms, tossing her into the air before catching her. She squealed in delight and wrapped her arms around his neck. "Let's move this to the bed. I want to play."

Tori giggled, feeling strangely carefree in his arms. Quinn bent to kiss her as he made his way across the room with tiny steps, his pants dragging around his ankles behind them.

Chapter Five

The next morning, Quinn was grinning like a fool before he awoke. Tori had been a little wildcat, and he could honestly say he was drained. Never had he had a lover who could keep up with and maybe even surpass him with her need. Oh, and was she a vixen! The things she could do with her mouth he'd only dreamt about. Thinking about it, he moaned. As his shaft rose to the memory of her lips on him, he knew that he'd been wrong. He was almost drained, almost.

She was adventurous too, allowing him to bend her however he wished without protest. They'd both been too eager to stop and play bed games, but he was sure she'd readily agree to them. With that in mind, his hand slid next to him on the silk sheets of the bed, reaching for her.

Quinn's fingers met with the mattress and he frowned. His head lifted, but not his body. Automatically, he knew she'd left him. Her presence wasn't in the room and he felt cold without it. A frustrated sigh left his mouth and his head dropped on the mattress. Damned but she was a frustrating woman!

* * * *

Tori looked out over the shadowed marshes. The four scientists were led on foot by two Var guards. Both Var men looked shyly at her with curious expressions, but none smiled as boldly as before. It was almost as if their attraction to her was tempered and she couldn't help but wonder if they knew about her and the prince's night together. She wasn't ashamed of her actions, but was concerned that it might affect the legitimacy of her presence there.

They all carried large hiking packs on their backs, all except the older Simon who carried a small bag over his shoulder. The bulk of their supplies would be brought up later that day, just as soon as they found the perfect place to camp. They were told that it was an hour of travel over rough terrain before they'd reach the caves.

As they'd left the palace, they passed the Var city. It was nestled in the valley below the castle. The city was a bustling maze of earthen streets and large rectangular homes, whose walls and foundation were constructed of fired bricks held together by mortar. Clay pots were set outside doorsteps, some with flowers and other native plants.

The streets were clean and orderly. Beautiful woven rugs and blankets hung outside in the sun, drying on lines. There was less intricate tile work than inside the palace, but the city was lovely nonetheless. Many of the homes were two stories high with flat roofs and no windows. The grand design indicated that most of the Var population prospered.

The sound of young boys playing echoed around them briefly as they passed the city, then all noise was swallowed up by the surrounding forest and marshland. Tori had caught a glimpse of the palace as they traveled. It stood tall against the blue-green sky. Square turrets reached high into the heavens, looming commandingly over the city. It was truly magnificent.

According to their guides, they trudged through the edge of the swamplands. The trees of the forest were huge, bigger than the legendary redwoods on earth. Tori felt dwarfed by them.

They were told to keep their feet from the murky waters, as a poisonous snake called a *givre* swam freely in them. Across the swamps to the north was the Draig palace. The guards tensed slightly when she asked about the Var's longtime enemy, but finally grudgingly admitted that the Draig had acted honorably so far and there was nothing to make them suspect they'd cause the scientists trouble--especially since they were there to make sure the biological weapons were completely gone.

A diffused light fell over the dense forest in a soft green haze that blended eerily with the patches of hot, steamy fog from the nearby marshes. From what Tori could tell, there wasn't much difference between the swamps and the marshes, except that the marshes seemed dead of all life.

The marshes were an awful place. Moss hung from treetops, unmoving in their windless isolation. The air was damp, stagnant, and filled with the rotting smell of molding plant life and animal carcasses. Even the insects seemed to have deserted the area.

Stopping, Tori shared a concerned look with Vitto. Quietly, she said, "This doesn't feel right."

Vitto nodded. Grant stopped near them, hearing her comment. He frowned, looking around as if for the first time that late morning. He'd been grumpy since he'd been pulled from Linzi's bed, and they'd left him alone for the most part. Now, a professional light entered his eyes, turning him serious. He slowly nodded in agreement of Tori and Vitto.

"Excuse me," Grant said to the guards, stopping them in their progress. "Have the marshes always been like this?"

"Have been since I can remember," one answered.

The other, who Tori sensed was the older, more hardened of the two, said, "You know, when I was a young boy we used to hunt here. There was wildlife all along the Western Ridges, but that was ages ago. Now this black moss grows on everything."

"Black moss?" Tori asked, looking around. She didn't see any black moss.

"Here," the guard offered. He walked over to a stone and kicked it over. Sure enough there was a black fungus on the bottom of it. As they watched, it slowly withered as if affected by the sunlight. Within a few seconds, it turned a dark gray.

"That's going to make it harder to study," Vitto observed.

"Hmm, not if we figure out if it's the air or the light that affects it," Simon put forth from behind them.

"Come on, guys," Tori urged. "Let's set up camp first, then we can begin collecting samples and mapping the cave systems."

"You know," Grant allowed as they began walking again. "You never mentioned how your date with Prince Quinn went."

Vitto began snickering. Tori stopped. She eyed Vitto and then Grant.

"What did you two do?" she demanded with a worried frown.

"Nothing," Vitto said, trying to look innocent and failing.

"Yeah, nothing," Grant mimicked.

"You better spill it," Tori warned.

"They told him you were a feminist and you hated to be treated like a lady," Simon offered with a sheepish grin.

Vitto and Grant laughed harder at their own joke.

"Come on, Elliot," Grant pleaded. "You have to tell us what happened. What did you say to the poor guy? We know you tore him apart."

"Come on, Tor! We've been dying to know." Vitto turned his dark eyes to her in merriment.

"Actually, you two troublemakers, he was a perfect gentleman," Tori announced. "He brought me flowers, chocolate and a bottle of wine. It would seem some men know how to treat a lady and how not to listen to morons like you!"

"Oh my gawd!" Grant announced. His mouth dropped open. "You got laid!"

"Ew!" Vitto grimaced. He grabbed his ears and started wailing. "I didn't want to hear that! My ears, my ears, they're burning! Make it stop, mommy, make it stop!"

Tori hit him repeatedly on the arm to make him be quiet.

"That's workplace abuse," he grumbled good-naturedly. "I'll take you up on a section eight charge."

"You're an imbecile," Tori said. "Section eight is for misappropriate use of funding. Now shut up or I'll tell everyone how you really got this job."

"You shut up or I'll tell everyone what I used to call you when we were kids," Vitto returned with an impish grin.

"Do and I'll fire you!" she teased.

"Tori," Vitto whined. He made a face behind her back as she walked away.

Grant laughed and, in a little kid voice, said, "*Ooooh!* You're gonna be in so much trouble, Vitto. I'm telling Dr. Elliot on you."

* * * *

"What do you mean, she left?" Quinn asked his brother in the growling tone of their shared language. Kirill looked up from his long stone desk in the royal office to study his brother. He was surrounded by chairs, a couch, and rugs.

The royal office was much like the rest of the palace with the same beautiful tile work on the walls and the same medieval castle feel to the structure. Opposite Kirill's desk, a large barren fireplace was dwarfed by the even larger sidewall. Long banners hung on either side of it. A large woven rug of red and blue lay on the floor. Its intricate pattern was perhaps the loveliest in the palace. Next to the rug were large chairs, so deep they'd nearly swallow a person whole.

"She insisted on going, to get started this morning. I'm having the rest of her supplies sent out after they established what she called a base camp. Why?" Kirill's nearly black eyes studied his brother curiously. "Has something happened? You seem oddly ... tense. It's unlike you."

"I'm fine," Quinn grouched. He paced around the office, stopping at the fireplace to look at nothing in particular.

"Ah, so it did not go so well last night, I take it?" Kirill asked, standing from his desk. "Did you give her the flowers?"

"Yes."

"The chocolate?"

"Yes. Yes. Yes," Quinn insisted. "I gave her ... everything."

"Ah," Kirill answered then, as a knowing look came to him. He said, "*Ooohh.* Then you're upset because she's gone."

"Ever since you fell in love you're really annoying, you know that," Quinn stated with a grimace. "My mood has nothing to do with Dr. Elliot leaving. I only wish to be informed of their whereabouts for the sake of my duty. I can't very well be ambassador if I don't know where the scientists are at all times, can I?"

Kirill ignored the question and chuckled instead. "Ever since you laid eyes on the female doctor, your moods have been very unpredictable. Women will do that to you."

"What, you've been married for two days and suddenly you're an expert on women? This coming from the man who thought calling a woman his property was a compliment." Quinn shook his head. It had taken Kirill a long time to come around to accepting his feelings for Ulyssa.

"My Lyssa knows what I mean, that's all that matters," Kirill answered with a grin and a shrug. "I am as much her property as she is mine."

"I am happy for you, brother," Quinn allowed. "She is a good woman and she will give you a fine son."

"Thank you."

Quinn moved to go.

"Quinn," Kirill called.

"Yeah?"

"You know, it wouldn't be so terrible if you found a good woman and mated to her." Kirill's voice was quiet, gauging. "It really does something to the inner self. I've never felt more whole."

"What would our father say to that? Two sons falling for women." Quinn chuckled, but even as he laughed, he heard his father's words drumming into his brain. "*To be ruled by a woman is to be ruled by weakness. Kingdoms are only as strong as their rulers, and you must be strong my sons. A man cannot bow to a woman and still call himself a man. To fall for a woman is to fall for stupidity.*"

"Attor was wrong," Kirill said softly when Quinn didn't move, didn't answer. "A woman's love gives strength not weakness."

"Until you lose it, brother," Quinn answered so softly Kirill couldn't hear. He wouldn't dampen his brother's happiness with his own doubts about love and mating. He was glad for the king, but knew such a thing as life mates and happiness wasn't for everyone. It most likely wouldn't be for him.

* * * *

Tori looked over the campsite and nodded in approval of it. They'd managed to set up four tents on relatively flat ground. A rocky cliff rose high on one side and the guards told her that was where the entrance to the cave system started.

Their supplies came a couple hours after they arrived and a fifth tent was set up as a makeshift laboratory. Grant and Vitto were unpacking the equipment and she could hear their mischievous arguing coming from inside the tent. She grinned as Vitto yelled. A loud smack sounded and Grant's cry of pain soon followed.

"Boys!" she yelled. "Don't make me separate you two!"

"Yes, mom!" came their cry in unison.

Tori chuckled and shook her head. "I'll be right back. I'm going to climb up to the cave."

A rope ladder hung from the entrance. It had been there when they arrived. Testing it out, she decided it appeared sturdy enough and began to climb.

"Hey, be careful!" Vitto yelled beneath her.

"I'm just checking out the entrance. I won't be long," she answered.

Tori made her way to the opening and crawled inside. She stood, glancing into the dim cave light. Grabbing a flashlight off her utility belt, she shone it around the opening. The stone was red, the color of the Qurilixen soil. Seeing a narrow tunnel toward the back, she moved toward it. She had to turn sideways to get through, but she managed it with little trouble.

The tunnel led to a large cavern. Crystal formations protruded from the ceiling. They reflected the outside light, causing spots to dance on the walls like little rainbows. Small inlets and tunnels spiraled off from the side walls. She turned off her light, not needing it. Then, grabbing a sticker off her utility belt, she peeled it back and slapped it on the wall, marking the exit with a big green circle.

After a quick walk through, Tori left the beautiful cave. Simon had started supper on the campfire when she reached the bottom. She grinned at him as he stirred a big pot.

"What we having tonight?" she asked.

"Stew," Simon chuckled.

"Ala something from a foil pack labeled stew," Grant offered, holding up the empty foil pack for her to see.

Tori laughed, before asking cautiously, "Does it look good?"

"It better be good," Vitto said as she came to sit by him on a long bench they'd found in the supplies. "It's the only thing we have. Five cases of nothing but stew and dehydrated coffee."

"Ugh," Tori grumbled. "You're kidding right? Please tell me you're kidding."

* * * *

Quinn was crazy. He knew it. He was walking through the marshland on foot to confront a woman he hardly knew to find out why she ran away from his bed. Yep, it was a crazy plan. A stupid plan. It was his plan.

He'd been walking for an hour, thinking about what lame excuse he'd use once he got to the campsite. Maybe, being as he was the ambassador, he wouldn't need an excuse to check in on her--them. Hearing voices, he stopped. Tori's laughter rang up around him and he couldn't help but smile to hear it.

"Does it look good?" Tori asked.

"It better be good," Vitto answered. "It's the only thing we have. Five cases of nothing but stew and dehydrated coffee."

Quinn came to the trees. His eyes narrowed as he saw Tori sitting close to Vitto on the bench. She leaned in to bump his shoulder with a playful nudge. Claws grew from his fingertips, ready to cut through Vitto's throat if she dared touch the man again.

"Ugh," Tori grumbled. "You're kidding right? Please tell me you're kidding."

"Not at all," Vitto answered. His arm reached around to give Tori a hug. Quinn gripped the trunk of a tree and dug in his claws as he fought a full shift. His nostrils flared and his jaw tightened painfully.

"Hey, knock it off you two!" Grant demanded. "You know the rules ... no affection unless I'm in on it."

"Oh, baby, come here and give mama some sugar!" Tori teased.

Quinn's hands balled into fist, scraping the bark from the tree. He forced his claws to retract. Taking a deep breath, he shook with outrage. But, instead of storming forward like he wanted to, he turned and stalked away.

* * * *

"Oh, baby, come here and give mama some sugar!" Tori teased Grant with a roll of her eyes.

Grant paused in his walk across the campsite and pointed a finger at her. "Don't tempt me, sugar mama. I just might crawl into your tent tonight and bite you on the ass!"

"Is that how you got Linzi into your bed?" Tori asked with a smirk. "With threats?"

Grant made a small noise and took a deep, dramatic breath before sighing loudly. "Oh, she was the only one doing the biting last night. I tell you what. She brought out these chains and a whip--"

"Oh!" Tori and Vitto grimaced in unison.

"Too much!" Tori shouted in laughter.

"My ears, my ears!" Vitto chimed in, taking his arms from Tori to put them over his ears.

"Quiet!" Simon demanded. They all looked at him with wide eyes, surprised at his harsh tone. He motioned for silence with a large spoon. "You two let the boy speak. This conversation was just getting good!"

The younger scientists rolled with laughter and Simon just grinned, moving back to stir his pot.

* * * *

After a few weeks being at the camp, they fell into a normal routine. In the mornings they would map out the caves and check for signs of contamination. The equipment HIA sent them was unable to sense through the rock, so they had to go to each cavern individually to search. It was a tedious process, but they were scientists and well used to tedious assignments.

In the late afternoons, they'd collect samples from the surrounding swamplands--water, soil, green and black moss. It was discovered that air is what killed the black moss, so loads of rock and dirt were hauled into the laboratory tent where they set up a special environment to test the strange fungus.

During their time, the four scientists had no contact with the outside world. They were used to the isolation, but for some reason it seemed to be wearing on Tori more than usual. At night, alone in her tent, she would relive each moment with Quinn in her head. It was only a few days, but it felt like a lifetime. The way he'd kissed her, made love to her, stayed in her thoughts during the day. At night, he haunted her dreams. There was no way around it. She missed him.

"Ah!" Tori yelled as mud splattered onto her face. A large clump got into her mouth, making her gag. "Oh, crap! Darn it! Crap! Crap! Crap!"

"Tori?" Vitto called, his voice giving away his concern. She heard the tent flap lift behind her. "What happened?"

"I-I got distracted," Tori answered, swiping mud from her eyes and spitting. She flicked her gloved hands in the air. "I wasn't paying attention to what I was doing and I got careless."

"Damn it, Tori, it's in your eyes!" Vitto moved away only to come back. She felt a cool rag on her face as Vitto swiped her clean. "This distraction has been happening a lot lately. Care to share?"

"No," she grumbled. "I just want to take a bath."

"Listen," Vitto began. "I've been thinking that it's about time we headed back to the palace to report to HIA, not to mention King Kirill. We're almost done with the caves, except for that lower subsystem Grant found yesterday in the east tunnel. I know you're in charge and we'll do what you decide, but it's just a friendly suggestion."

"Grant just wants to see Linzi," Tori answered, chuckling. She'd honestly been putting off going back to the palace, though she knew Vitto was right. They did need to check in with HIA and report. And it never hurt to keep the locals informed of their progress. It also made for good relations when and if they needed to stay longer than planned.

"And you want a bath and I want to eat something besides that horrible dehydrated, 'I'm sure the Agency really just wanted to kill us with it anyway' stew."

"I know. I think we're all at least fifty pounds lighter since this began," Tori chuckled, tired. She could use a bed and a warm bath. Slowly, she nodded. "All right. Have everyone secure our site so we can go. We'll leave in about an hour and a half for the Var palace."

* * * *

When the four weary scientists trudged into the palace, they were greeted by the king. He smiled at them, not seeming surprised that they were there. Tori guessed the guards had alerted him before they even made the edge of the Var city. After a brief report to Kirill and Falke about their progress, they were allowed to go back to their rooms to rest.

Tori searched for Quinn, as she made her way back to her suite, but didn't see him. She was almost afraid to face him, scared of what he thought of her. She'd acted completely wanton and she'd been too nervous to face him in the light of morning. He hadn't tried to contact her since she left, though she secretly longed for him to. There were many nights she laid alone in her tent, wishing and praying he'd come to her, even if it was for one night.

Now that she was back in the suite, the memories of Quinn flooded her anew. Her body heated, curling with the beginnings of desire. Humming a twentieth century earth tune, Tori stretched her legs across the bathtub. The curtains were drawn over the windows, leaving the bath dim. Water was so much better than trying to clean with a hand sanitizer in the cool air of morning out in the forest. Rubbing soap over her skin, she washed at leisure, daydreaming that it was Quinn's hands on her body.

"Want some company?"

Tori jolted in surprise. The words materialized as if out of her thoughts. She turned in the bath to see Quinn standing below the platform. An instant blush stained her features and she swallowed almost nervously. She hoped the steam from the water made her looked flushed so he wouldn't notice. He looked tired, but gorgeous. Just seeing him took her breath away. Her heart leapt.

"Quinn," she panted, breathless. "You're ... here."

"Kirill told me you were back." Without waiting for her permission, he began undressing. It seemed natural that he would do so and she didn't protest. Tori watched him as his beautiful body was unveiled.

"What are you doing?" she asked belatedly, as he stepped up to the tub. His body was erect, ready for her, and she grew excited just knowing it.

"I figured I'd come help you relax," he answered, giving her a small grin.

Tori studied him carefully. There was something different about him, but it was hard to name. It was his eyes. They didn't seem so bright a blue. And his smile, it didn't appear so mischievous in intent.

"Is-is something the matter?" she asked as he came up next to her. "You look stressed. Are you having problems with the Draig? With Lord Myrddin? Has something happ--"

"How was your work?" he interrupted, instead of answering. Taking the rag from her hand, he lathered it up and motioned for her to turn around. She did and he began washing her back.

Tori moaned. His strong hand felt as good as she remembered along her skin, easing the tension from her muscles. She loved his hands.

"Work was fine," she answered at length. "We think we've got the caves almost cleared, though we really didn't expect to find much."

"And our neat Var marshland mud?" he asked.

She glanced over her shoulder and he winked at her.

"It's still neat," she returned, laughing. "I wanted to ask you about the black moss though. Like, where'd it come from? How--?"

"*Shhh*, later. We'll discuss it later." He leaned in to lick at her earlobe.

"Mmmm," she moaned, instantly forgetting about work and black moss.

"So, did you miss me?" he questioned, dropping the cloth and rubbing his hands around to her front to glide around her large breasts.

Tori wasn't sure how to answer, so she just made a weak sound. Yes, she had missed him--terribly.

His hot breath hit against her ear, as he came up along her back and pressed his body along hers. Heatedly, he whispered, "Did you miss this?"

"*Ahhh*," she panted, weak.

He pulled her tight against his kneeling frame, so she could feel the heavy length of him in full detail. His soapy fingers pinched her nipples into hard buds, massaging the weight in firm strokes. She arched back into him, running her hands behind her head to touch his silken hair. Her fingers tangled in the locks, pulling him closer.

The warm probing lick of his tongue found her ear. It swirled around the outside rim, making her shiver with anticipation. After showing the lobe the same thorough attention, his kisses moved to her neck. He lightly nipped at her flesh until it stung pleasurably.

Quinn's hand slid down her stomach, moving to settle between her thighs. His finger parted the lips of her body, gliding forward to stroke her tender flesh. She shivered, crying out in ecstasy. She'd missed him so much. It was hard to explain, but she had. He'd been the best lover she'd ever been with, making her orgasm so many times she'd nearly lost consciousness. The idea that he would do so again caused her to turn around in his arms.

Tori paused, looking deeply into his blue eyes. It felt as if no time had passed since they last touched. She leaned forward, kissing him, rolling her tongue between his lips to massage the velvet heat of his mouth.

Her hands explored his body, gliding over his arms and chest, playing along his nipples, curving down to stroke his hard stomach and sides. She pulled her mouth from his to explore the taste of his neck, his shoulders. She couldn't feel enough of him as she rediscovered his body's secrets. When her hand moved between them to take his length into her palm, he let loose a loud moan into the suite. The warm water of the bath made her fingers glide with ease.

Tori stroked him, moving to cup the soft globes underneath as she ran her fingers up and down over his shaft beneath the surface. If not for the water, she'd have taken him in her mouth. She remembered well how much he liked it when she did that, how much she liked doing it for him.

"Ah, Tori," he groaned softly, thrusting his hips up. "Sacred Cats, woman! You drive me mad."

Pleasure rolled through her as she continued to kiss him. His hands were on her back, her breasts, searching down to explore between her moist thighs. Lightly, he circled a finger over the sensitive nub he found buried in her wet, hot depths. The warm water only made his exploration all the more gratifying.

Eagerly, his hands found her hips and he lifted her body astride his. Without pause, he pulled her onto him, impaling his shaft deep within her as he pried into her ready body. Water splashed around her waist, rocking in waves between them. She watched his eyes shift to green ecstasy. The threat of his shifted form thrilled her, made her heart leap inside the walls of her chest.

"Ah, you feel so damn good," he groaned, throwing his head back to rest along the tub's rim. His hands stayed on her hips, as he lifted and pulled her in very shallow, very gentle strokes. "So tight. So ... hot. Damn, woman, every time I see you I nearly explode with need."

Tori shivered. She braced her hands on his shoulders and pulled up. His hands on her hips followed her as she moved. When he was almost out of her, he pulled her down hard. They both groaned. This time, Quinn pushed her up fast and pulled her down again, repeating the hard motion.

Their primitive instincts took over and she began to ride him. Her breasts bobbed before him and he eagerly thrust his face between her large breasts, smothering a moan of enjoyment in the valley of them as they worked up and down over his cheeks. His hands grabbed the heavy globes, rolling the nipples, drawing them over so they'd pass by his tongue as she moved. She loved his fascination with her breasts.

Tori screamed in approval. Her body moved faster, the movements becoming shallow strokes. The tension built between them, driving them harder as they neared release. He felt so good, so big and strong. Quinn's mouth latched onto her breast and he sucked a hard nipple deep into his mouth. His thumb moved over her stomach to find the sensitive nub, rubbing it in small hard circles, as she thrust herself harder and faster.

"Oh my, Quinn!" she screamed. Quinn bit down on the sensitive nipple between his teeth and answered with a throaty groan. "Quinn, oh, yes, there, baby, oh... oh ... don't stop! Don't stop! Oh, baby, please don't stop! You feel good, oh you feel good. Right there, baby, right there. That's it. I'm coming. I'm com ... *ah!*"

Tori cried out, throwing her head back, as she thrust her body hard onto his. Tremors racked her, shaking her to the core. Quinn groaned as she took her pleasure, her convulsing body spurring him to do the same. His seed spurted inside her and, for a long moment, they were completely connected.

Tori dropped weakly along his body and a purring noise sounded in the back of her throat. Her eyes closed and she rested against him, so relaxed she almost fell asleep in his arms. "*Mm*, Quinn."

Quinn leaned over to look at her beautiful features. Dark circles purpled beneath her eyes, giving way to the fact that she'd been working hard and nonstop. He'd sent guards out to check on the scientists, unable to force himself to go back. Even now, after weeks had passed, jealousy reared its ugly head inside him.

When the guards reported her return to the palace, he'd sworn to himself that he wasn't going to see her. Or, if he did, he was going to act nonchalant. He stood around the corner, listening to the report she gave Kirill. Just the sound of her low, professional voice had stirred his blood and in that moment he knew he could no longer stay away from her than he could live without air in his lungs. He just had to see her.

The palace had become a dismal place without her in it. How it happened in such a short time, he'd never know. He missed her, fantasized about her--and not just about sex, though he did have those thoughts aplenty. He fantasized about her soft laugh, about the light noise she made when she was nervous, or the strange tunes he'd heard her hum when she was preoccupied. He was sure she didn't even know she did it.

Or like how in bed she liked it when he stroked to the left just a little harder than the right. How sensitive her breasts were and how she enjoyed it when he bit at them. How she was the most vocal woman he'd ever brought to climax-- which did great things for any man's ego. Not once did she get all shy about it, worrying about who might have heard her. All that he'd learned in just a few short days of knowing her. All that was permanently committed to his memory.

As her chest rose and fell in even breaths, he smiled. She was asleep, her arms draped over his neck. Carefully, he stood. Tori mumbled in light protest as he lifted her from the tub. Then, pulling a towel from nearby he tried to dry them both off. Her eyes opened lazily and she grinned at him, a catlike smile that drove him to distraction.

"Why don't you carry me to the bed?" she murmured, content to lean against him. "I don't think I can walk."

Quinn chuckled and easily lifted her into his arms. Laying her on the bed, he drew the covers over them and pulled her into the cradle of his body.

"You're not going to take off again, are you?" he asked, almost hesitant. Her eyes were closed and she couldn't see the vulnerable look that crossed his features.

Lazily, she opened one eye to look him over. "Are you just going to lay there cowboy, or are you going to saddle up?"

Quinn frowned, confused. "Cowboy?"

"Mm, never mind, I'll have to explain the concept later." Tori lifted her arms around his neck and a soft chuckle escaped her. "It could be fun."

"Then you must definitely explain it to me," Quinn murmured.

Tori was still sleepy, but her body had warmed to the idea of making love to him again--this time slower. Her fingers roamed aimlessly along the deep contours of his chest. "Why don't you be on top this time?"

Quinn didn't have to be asked twice. He maneuvered his hips between hers, rotating to lie on top of her. He made love to her slowly, savoring her body with his mouth and hands. His lips latched onto her heated center, bringing her to climax with his exploring tongue and lips. And, as the shivers of it still racked her, he lifted himself and entered her in slow, deep strokes, keeping the sensation alive.

Tori loved the look of him above her, of his graceful, streamlined body. She liked how his muscles moved and bent beneath his flesh as he thrust his hard length inside her. Her arms moved lazily, nearly too exhausted to lift up to him. But it felt too good. She never wanted him to stop.

Quinn brought her again to climax. It was a gentle washing of tremors compared to the hard force they experienced in the bath. He drew out the bittersweet moment so the pleasure lasted a long time. Finally, he let go, releasing his seed into her, letting his body lay his claim on her, marking her as his. She was already marked by him, though she didn't know it. This time, he'd make damned sure she couldn't take another man to her bed--not Vitto, not Grant, not anyone.

"Tori," he whispered down to her drowsy face. Her eyes fluttered open, and she made soft sounds of contentment.

"*Mmmm*, you feel so good. Just stay right there, deep inside me. It feels so good," she murmured sleepily. "I wish I could stay awake to do it again, but I'm just so exhausted."

"Tori, listen to me," he insisted in a hurried whisper. Her tired eyes looked at him. "You are mine."

"*Mmmm*, all right Quinn, yours," she mumbled before falling into a deep sleep.

Chapter Six

Tori yawned and reached up to scratch her face. It was early morning, but she'd always been an early riser. Frowning, she kept scratching. Her skin felt like it was on fire. Quinn's arm possessively draped around her waist, his hand holding one of her breasts. His fingers twitched slightly in his sleep. A light smile crossed her features as she gently pried his hand away. He mumbled in protest and she stiffened. Then, as he flipped onto his back, she was able to slide off the bed undetected.

Again frowning as her irritated skin demanded attention, she rushed to the full length mirror. Standing before it naked, she froze in horror. Her face and neck were covered in large, patchy, red bumps and they itched unbearably.

"I look deformed," she whispered in horror. Her heart dropped from her chest. Tori was completely mortified. She glanced back to the bed where the prince slept, knowing she couldn't let Quinn see her like this--not like this!

Tori ran to her pack and threw on a black jumpsuit and lab coat. Not bothering with her hair, she ran from the suite. Using the lab coat and hair to hide her features, she hurried past a few of the guards. She was very thankful when they let her by without comment. Reaching Vitto's door, she pounded on it. It took awhile, but he finally answered.

"Um?" he mumbled, half asleep. Rubbing his eyes, he looked out in the hall and grimaced. "Man, Tori, come on. It's too early to--"

Tori dropped the coat.

"Crap!" Vitto exclaimed, recoiling in shock.

"We gotta go now!" she hissed. "I'm heading back to the camp. Get everyone up and meet me there. There's something wrong with those samples we took and I'm going to find out what."

"But, Tori," he began, reaching for her then reconsidering as he pulled his hand back, "your face."

Tears welled in her eyes. Hissing between her teeth, she growled, "I know. Just meet me back at the camp, okay? I can't be seen like this!"

Vitto nodded. Leaning out into the hall, he watched in amazement as she ran away.

* * * *

Quinn's body shook with outrage before he even opened his eyes. He knew she was gone--sensed it before he even reached across the bed. His hand balled into a fist and he slammed it down hard on the mattress.

"Sacred Cats! She did it again," he hissed, partly in disbelief.

Tan fur filled in his body. His eyes dilated and shifted to a pale greenish yellow. Claws stretched from his fingernails and toenails as his hands and feet became thick paws. A roar left his parted lips as they pulled wide, elongating as his body shifted into the form of a cougar.

With a leap, he tore off of the bed and it didn't take long for him to work the doorknob with his paws. Rage blinded him to reason. Running down the hall on all fours, he passed Kirill.

The king blinked in surprised and yelled, "Quinn! What...?"

Quinn ignored him. He tore out of the front of the palace and disappeared into the gigantic forest.

* * * *

"Hold still, Tori," Vitto growled under his breath. "I'm almost done."

"What is it?" she asked, as he finished running the medical laser over her face.

"It appears just to be a rash of some sort. What sample were you working with?" Vitto turned to grab an electronic clipboard.

"The ones we collected from the south section a few days ago." Tori stood and touched her face. It felt like it was back to normal.

"You're still a little red and patchy," Vitto admitted, "but it should go away in a few days. You're lucky it wasn't a lot worse. I don't want you working with samples until your head is straight. It's not safe."

Before Tori could dispute him, Grant's voice came through the tent. "Uh, guys, you should see this."

They turned to Grant. His tanned face was pale as he solemnly motioned them to follow. Tori and Vitto shared a concerned look before moving to the tent flap.

"What's going on?" Tori asked, as Grant grabbed up a pack and moved to the ladder leading to the caves. Seeing Simon watching them, Tori stated, "We'll be right back, Simon."

"I'll start lunch," Simon answered as he nodded. Since he was older, Tori hated to make him climb the rope ladder. Besides, he was better in the lab than in the field anyway and he seemed to enjoy cooking for the team.

"I ... you just got to see it for yourself." Grant quickly climbed the ladder up into the cave. Leading the way through the tunnel to the main cavern, he paused. "When we were at the palace, well Linzi just finished--"

"Grant," Tori stated, not wanting the details at the moment.

Grant cleared his throat. "Well, anyway, you know I think best after sex, 'cause my head's the clearest. Anyway, something's really been bugging me about this new lower subsystem I found in the east tunnel."

Taking off his pack, Grant handed them each a mask. He moved to the east tunnel and pointed to the hole in the cave floor.

"Look at the opening. See how it looks chiseled more than formed by erosion? And, look at this. The rim's covered with that same black moss, only it's not dying in the air. I know that wasn't there before when I found this entrance." Grant pulled out gloves and handed them all round. Avoiding the moss along the edge of the opening, he hopped down into the hole. There was a sound of movement before his light shined up.

Tori and Vitto followed him into the hole. As Grant led the way, the moss became thicker and longer. Tori's boot splashed in a shallow pool of liquid, but she ignored it and kept going. The light became dim and it was hard to see as they made their way along the rocky cave system.

"Look," Grant whispered, pointing his light forward. "I think whatever is behind there is the source of the black moss."

An iron door was fitted into the wall of the cave. Tori gasped in amazement to see it. "What's a door doing down here?"

"I don't know," Vitto whispered. "But it looks old, just check out the hinges. They're rusted. I don't think anyone has been down here for a very long time."

"Let's open it and find out," Grant said, his words edged with scientific excitement.

They all knew it was a little careless to proceed, but no one stopped him from reaching forward. There was always a certain amount of risk in what they did. Tori felt Vitto's shoulder next to hers. He nodded at her before turning his attention back to the door. She adjusted the mask over her features, making sure she had a tight seal.

After a short struggle, Grant pulled the door open. Light flooded them from within. Tori blinked, letting her eyes adjust as Grant took a cautious step forward.

"Motion light sensors," Grant said, switching off his flashlight. "Whoever was here must have left them connected."

"Whoever it was, they haven't been back in awhile," Tori added.

Black moss covered nearly everything--tables, chairs, an antiquated computer system with a keyboard and desktop monitor. Only peeks of the equipment and part of the metal floor showed through.

"It's an old laboratory," Tori said. "What do you think they were doing down here?"

"By the looks of it, it's about a hundred or two hundred years old. All the computer files are probably corrupted by now." Vitto frowned. "But, one thing's for sure. Whatever this black moss is, it came from in here."

"Guys, look," Grant had wandered forward and they rushed to join him. He'd found a couple locked cages with piles of humanoid bones as if whatever was locked inside had just laid down and died. "Do you think they could have starved?"

"Possible," Vitto answered. "This place looks abandoned, not shut down. I mean, look," he pointed to a desk. "Personal belongings are scattered everywhere. You can see the outline of a file and papers right there."

"Okay, here's what we do," Tori instructed. She looked at the desk and seeing a long oval, picked it up and swept the moss from it to study it. On a whim, she shoved it into her pocket. "Grab whatever you can that might have some information on it. The Var palace mainframe is a little outdated so this stuff might still be salvageable. I want to figure out just what in the galaxy they were doing down here. Whatever this moss is, it started here and it's slowly poisoning this planet. The marshes are already dead. And, by the looks of the moss in the cave, it's mutating to survive in air. It could be nothing or we could have an ecological disaster on our hands."

* * * *

When Tori climbed down the ladder from the cave, it was to find her camp being torn apart by a group of Var soldiers. She frowned, as she saw Commander Falke order the dismantling of her tent. Her mouth opened to protest, but she was interrupted.

"Where have you been? I have guards combing the marshes for your dead bodies!"

Tori froze. She turned around. Quinn marched up to her wearing one of their lab coats. His bare feet and calves peaked out the bottom. Remembering what she looked like when she left him, she unconsciously lifted her hand to touch her face. She was relieved to find her skin smooth.

"Combing the marshes?" she repeated, frowning. "Why ... what's going on here? What's happened? Are you fighting again with the Draig? Why are you dismantling my tent? And what's that guy doing with my samples! It took us two weeks to get them collected and organized. He can't carry them together like that. Oh, he's contaminating them with...."

Tori made a move to go after a guard who roughly carried her samples of marsh mud. The little containers jingled and fell over, mixing together. Quinn's hand shot out and gripped her elbow, jerking her back.

Her mouth opened, but before she could speak, Vitto yelled down from the cave. "What's going on down there, Tor? Are we going to move this stuff down today or what?"

Quinn frowned up at the man, not letting go of her arm. Looking at Falke, he said, "Help them out."

Falke nodded and motioned to some guards to climb the ladder.

Tori gasped, as Quinn dragged her along to the forest. When they were alone, he turned to study her.

"Are you wearing my lab coat?" she asked, her brow arching in slight amusement. "And are you naked underneath it? What's going on here, Quinn? I don't understand."

"Are you harmed?" Quinn demanded ignoring her questions. His eyes roamed over her, not with pleasure, but fearfully searching her for injury.

"Harmed?" she repeated, confused.

"Damn it woman! Would you actually answer a question instead of just repeating it back to me?"

"W-wait," Tori stuttered, fighting her anger. Her finger lifted and she pointed it at him. "You storm in here and start tearing apart my camp and you think to ask me questions? What in the hell is going on, Quinn?"

"We thought you were injured. After we found Simon--"

"Simon?" Tori repeated. The blood rushed from her face. "What's wrong with Simon?"

"You weren't in hiding?"

"Hiding? I was working!" Tori panted, feeling sick. "What's wrong with Simon?"

"Tori, I'm sorry.... He's dead." Quinn frowned. Her dark eyes widened and she slowly shook her head.

"That's not possible," she whispered, beginning to shake. "He-he was just making lunch.... He's my responsibility. He can't be dead. We were only in the cave for just a couple hours at most. How...?"

"He was ... mauled," Quinn answered. He shifted his weight uncomfortably on his feet. His heart was still lodged in his throat and he wanted to pull her to his chest to make sure she was all right. He didn't know what he'd do if something happened to her.

Quinn had been so angry when he left the palace for the campsite. He'd stayed shifted in his cougar form as he sprinted to confront her. Then, he'd smelled the unmistakable hint of blood in the forest. In a panic, he'd found Simon's body, but he couldn't find the others. He'd checked the marshes, the forest, the opening of the cave and couldn't detect their scent. He had no choice but to run back to the palace and get help. Now, looking at her red-splotched face, he worried anew.

"Mauled?" she repeated, blinking in confusion. "As if by a cat?"

Quinn held up his hands. "I know what you're thinking Tori, but we had nothing to do with this. Let's just get you back to the palace where it's safe and then we'll talk about it. I promise you we'll find out what happened."

"Where's his body?" she demanded. "I want proof! I want to see his body!"

"Tori, please." Quinn reached for her.

She swatted him away and took a step back. "What are you even doing here Quinn?"

"I'm helping you. Tori, I promise, we'll discover who did this."

"No," she shot, her tone hard. Her eyes dried and she stiffened her lips. "*We* will figure this out. That's why we're here. To figure out exactly what is happening on this planet of yours. Simon was one of ours. If anyone will figure it out, we will. Since your soldiers have obviously carted off the better part of my camp, we will follow you back to the palace. But I want Simon's body untouched until we get there. I, along with my team, will examine him to determine the cause of death."

"Tori, wait," Quinn began when she would walk away. She turned to look at him, her face hard. "What about us?"

"Us," she snorted, shaking her head as if it was the stupidest thing she'd ever heard. "There is no 'us', Quinn. I never should have mixed business with pleasure. But, you can rest assured that it won't be happening again. All it did was make this situation more complicated than it needs to be. Now you must excuse me, my prince. I have to go inform my men about our loss."

Quinn said no more, watching her go. He felt as if she'd stabbed him in the chest. He was nothing but a complication to her. The realization was almost too hard to bear. He waited for his heart to stop beating, so that he may fall dead upon the ground. When the ache only grew worse, he forced his legs to move after her. Like it our not, she'd have his help. It was his duty as ambassador to give it.

* * * *

Tori took a long, slow drink of whiskey, glad the food simulator was able to materialize the hard liquor for her. It'd been a rough day. When Quinn said Simon's body had been mauled, he'd been kind in his assessment to her. In truth, there was little of it left for her and the guys to study.

She took another drink, choking down the burning liquid. They'd examined Simon, ran tests on him to try and discover who or what would do such a horrible thing. She'd made the necessary reports to ESC and HIA. They had DNA sequencing started on samples taken from the corpse, but it would be a few days before anything was conclusive. They would be able to narrow down the species, but not the exact person unless they compiled a list of suspects and took samples from each one. Problem was, the killer wouldn't just hand them the evidence willingly. They'd have to take it. Until they figured out who was Simon's murderer, the black moss project was put on hold.

Tori signed. Unbidden, Quinn entered her slightly drunken thoughts. She wished he was there to comfort her. They hadn't spoken since the forest, and she'd almost instantly regretted her harsh words. Grief had overwhelmed her with the need to strike out and he'd been the closest thing. She honestly didn't want to believe that there was nothing between them, for she felt something when she was with him--something raw and powerful and so very real. What she didn't know was if he felt it too.

It was a stinging connection inside her that called to him, recognized him from that first moment their eyes met in the hall. Just the memory of that first meeting made her sick with jealousy. His lips had been pressed to Linzi's. She'd been shocked to see them thus, but even more than that, she'd been envious. It had taken her awhile to recognize the emotion, but there it was--made suddenly clear now by the haze of hard earth liquor.

Hearing a knock on her suite door, Tori threw back the rest of her drink and wobbled to her feet. Unsteady, she stumbled across the palace suite to the door and threw it open. Quinn stood before her and she blinked to make sure he was really there.

"Tori, listen. I came to say I was sorry about Simon." He held a flower out for her. "I know it's not much, but I remembered earth women liked flowers."

Tori looked at the pale solarflower and then back at Quinn. Oh, but he was handsome. She could stare at him all day. Her hand didn't move to take the gift. Words welled up inside her, bursting to be free. There was so much she wanted to tell him at that moment, so much she wanted to confess. Her lips parted, held open for an instant before she said, "My face is deformed because of mud and I can't feel my teeth."

Quinn frowned in confusion. Tori shrugged. Then, her eyes rolling in her head, she fell forward, completely passed out.

* * * *

"What's wrong with her?" Quinn demanded, looking at Vitto in concern. He was careful to keep his eyes on the man as he stepped into Tori's suite. Tori was lying on the bed where he'd left her. Her actions scared him and her words had made no sense. Without a clue what to do with her, he had ordered the palace computer to fetch one of the human scientists, hoping he would be able to help her. Vitto was the one who came to the call. "She was talking incoherently and making odd noises right before she fell limp."

To his surprise, Vitto didn't go straight to Tori, but instead to an empty glass sitting on the table. The man had been sleeping when the prince summoned him and his short, tousled hair stood on end. His tired eyes narrowed, as he lifted the glass up to his nose and sniffed. Flinching slightly, he pulled it back.

"Whiskey." Vitto stated with a heavy sigh. He moved over toward Tori. "It's nothing to worry about. She's just drunk--very, very drunk. Today was hard on all of us, but most of all her. Simon was her responsibility and he died on her watch."

"The man's death is not her fault," Quinn defended quickly, frowning as he came forward. He kept a sharp eye on Vitto, watching as the man leaned over to feel Tori's forehead.

"You don't understand Tori then," the man chuckled sadly. "She'd never agree with that. She was put in charge and, in her eyes, she failed."

"And you think to understand her so well?" Quinn demanded, before he could stop himself. He saw Vitto's eyes soften with kindness, as he pushed back Tori's dark hair.

Vitto looked up at him, his gaze narrowing as he studied the Var prince. Slowly, he nodded, "Yes, yes I do."

Quinn's jaw stiffened. He wanted to punch something--anything. His fists clenched lightly at his sides. Vitto turned back to Tori and arranged her limbs on the bed. She mumbled, but didn't awaken.

"I'll stay with her tonight," Vitto said, not turning around to look at Quinn. "You can go ahead and go. There's nothing more we can do for her."

"No," the prince answered without thought. "I'll stay. You can go."

Vitto blinked, looking directly at him. "I'm afraid I can't allow that. She's unconscious."

"And why would she be safer with you?" Quinn charged. "I'm her lover. I should take care of her."

Vitto coughed, nearly choking on his own spit at the bold statement. His face paled and he looked at Tori and then to the Var prince. His mouth opened and then closed. Slowly, he nodded his head. "Fine. We both stay."

"Fine," Quinn growled. He made a move toward the bed. Vitto held up his hand to stop him.

"I think we both should stay over there." Vitto pointed at the long couch.

Quinn glared at him, but finally nodded in agreement. Going to Tori, he brushed her hair back down the way it was before Vitto moved it and leaned over to kiss her forehead. Her skin was warm beneath his lips, but she didn't move. He lightly touched a pale red patch on her cheek and frowned. Glancing over his shoulder, he saw Vitto watched with shaded eyes.

"She said mud did this?" Quinn prompted.

"She had an accident in the lab yesterday before we came back. Some of the swamp mud she was testing splashed up into her face. The rash didn't show up until this morning, but it's looking much better than it did." Vitto's expression eased, though it was still guarded. "It's why we went back to camp so fast."

Quinn nodded, letting his expression stay blank. Inside, his heart started to beat wildly. Maybe she'd only left him because she had to, not because she wanted to.

"You can sit there all night staring at her, but she's not going anywhere," Vitto said softly. "And she won't hear anything you have to say."

Quinn nodded, tucked the blanket around her shoulders, and moved to the floor before the fire. He began stripping out of his clothes. Vitto gave him a funny look and cleared his throat.

"Ah, what are you doing?" Vitto asked, slightly distressed.

"You may have the couch. I'll take the floor," Quinn stated, wondering what was wrong with the human, as he pulled off his pants, baring his body. Vitto made a strange noise and when Quinn glanced at him, he was looking at the ceiling in discomfort.

The prince shook his head. Letting the tingling of the cougar shift come over his body, he heard Vitto gasp as the transformation took place. Tan fur rippled his skin and he soon stood on all fours. It would be a lot more comfortable sleeping on the floor as a cat than as a man. When he turned, Vitto stared at him with his jaw dropped.

Quinn frowned, guessing it must be a human thing and that's why he didn't understand what made Vitto so out of it. Yawning, his wide jaw stretched wide to bare his sharp teeth. The prince arched his back up into the air, stretching his tired muscles before settling for the night.

As he lay down, he sensed Vitto relaxing. His voice weak, the man said, "Ah, good night then, Prince Quinn."

Quinn lifted his head and nodded once, letting a small roar come from his throat. He couldn't speak the human words with his cat voice. Vitto gulped and waved lightly before lying down on the couch.

Chapter Seven

Tori felt terrible, but a pounding headache didn't keep her from rolling out of bed early the next morning. Stumbling barefoot across the floor, she went to the food simulator and materialized a glass of water. Then, going to her bag, she pulled out a handheld medic unit, fumbled with the knob, and then gave herself a shot in the neck. Almost instantly the tension eased and she could function, though her body still felt a little weak.

She was a little surprised to discover Vitto on the couch sleeping, but even more so to see the large cougar on the floor. At her gasp, the big cat opened its pale green eyes and looked at her. Coming to her on all fours, the cat nudged her hand playfully, cupping his nose into her palm. The fur was soft and she couldn't help but stroke it as she absently rubbed along his jaw and throat. There was something familiar about the cat and she was unafraid.

Sighing, she said, "I don't even want to know what you're doing sleeping naked on the floor, Quinn, but maybe you should get dressed before Vitto wakes up."

The face next to her began to shift and change. Fur was replaced by flesh, and Quinn's eyes turned to a bright blue to gaze up at her. A look of amazement crossed his features. Tori shivered. He really was too handsome for words.

"You knew me," he said, awed.

"Of course I knew you, Prince. You're a race of cat shifters." Tori grimaced. Then, placing her hand to her temple, she took a small drink of water and turned to the bath. Over her shoulder, she added, "Besides, I'm a scientist. I used logic. Your clothes are crumpled on the floor by the couch."

Tori ordered the bath to fill, as she drew the curtains completely around the tub for privacy. When she finished, she found Quinn wearing his pants but nothing else. A grin curled the side of his firm mouth, as he glanced suggestively toward the tub. Tori shook her head in denial.

"No, I think you need to go. I have a lot of work to do. Besides, Vitto's here." Tori placed her hands on her hips and waited for him to leave.

Quinn's features fell, as he glanced at Vitto then back to her. He crossed his arms over his chest and stated, "If he stays, I stay. I'm not leaving you alone with him."

"Excuse me?" Tori demanded, not in the mood to fight. What was his problem anyway? "I'm perfectly safe with Vitto. Besides, he's asleep."

"He can wake up," Quinn countered. An unreasonable stubbornness crossed over his face. "And you will be in the bath."

"So?"

Quinn's face hardened and turned red with anger. He shook and she stumbled backward.

"I think I have more to fear from you than him," Tori stated. Quinn's nostrils flared. "Besides, I've been camping in the wood with him and two other men almost every night since I've been here. If anything was going to happen with any one of them, it would have happened."

Remembering Simon, she paled. Quinn didn't speak.

"Just get out, Quinn. I can't do this now. I'm tired and I don't want to fight with you." Tori disappeared behind the curtains. She felt a tear slip down her cheek. She hadn't allowed herself to cry over Simon and waves of grief surged over her, drowning her in sorrow.

"Tori?" Quinn's voice asked. The anger was gone from his words, replaced by concern. "Tori, can I...?"

"I'll talk to you later, Prince," she answered, refusing to let the tears into her voice. She had to stay strong. She was in charge and she refused to let him see her cry. It was important that she keep a professional front until she figured out what was happening. Already, her life had gotten too complicated.

The sound of the door opening and shutting invaded her thoughts. She felt even more alone knowing Quinn was gone. Tori forced her limbs to move, quickly undressing as she crawled into the bath. When she was clean, she wrapped a towel around her body and moved to cross the suite to her bag. Vitto was awake, sitting on the couch when she came out of the curtained area.

"Drink the demons down?" he asked lightly.

Tori chuckled darkly, changing her course for the couch. She adjusted the large towel around her body, completely covering herself from view.

"Prince Quinn was here," Vitto said when she didn't answer.

Tori slid on the couch next to him and laid her head on his shoulder. "I know. I saw him."

"Care to tell me how long you've been lovers? Grant and I were only teasing about it. We didn't actually think you slept with him." Vitto nudged her lightly. "I don't have to tell you that it's a mistake to get involved with royalty, do I?"

"No," Tori mumbled.

"And that it's stupid to mix business and pleasure?"

"No."

"Hmm, well then," Vitto lifted his arm to settle around her shoulders. "Am I safe to assume he's the reason you've been distracted?"

"No." The lie was obvious and they both began to chuckle, though the sound was humorless and sad. "Yes."

"How serious is it?" Vitto ran his hand comfortingly over her arm.

"I ended it," she answered. "It's over. With Simon's death, I can't be involved with anyone from this planet, let alone a Var prince. I don't want to be blind and I can't have my judgment in this matter come into question."

"He cares about you, Tor," Vitto insisted. "That much is clear. And we would never question your judgment."

"Nothing will come of it. Besides, work first, play later. You know that. And right now I have more work than I can handle. We should have a team of at least twenty scientists working on this problem, not three."

"We've dealt with worse," Vitto said softly. "We'll deal with this."

"So, what did he say about me?"

"I thought it was over."

"It is." Tori hit him lightly in the side, but didn't lift up her head. "Now, tell me what he said."

"It was more how he looked at you," Vitto answered. "And he refused to leave me alone with you last night."

Tori laughed at the very idea that something would have happened. Vitto's chuckle joined hers.

"That's just gross," Tori snorted.

"Agreed," Vitto answered. "But, very ... ah, sweet on his part."

"No, it's just his Neanderthal way of marking territory. Kind of like an animal peeing on a tree trunk." Tori sat up. "I can guarantee a man like that hasn't been sleeping alone while I was gone. When I first met him he was in the hall making out with Linzi."

"Grant's Linzi?" Vitto snickered.

"One and the same," Tori admitted. She stood to get dressed, moving onto the bed so she was hidden from view. Vitto didn't try to look, but kept his eyes on the fireplace.

"Don't tell Grant that. He's convinced he's rocked that woman's world." Vitto chuckled again, before suppressing a yawn.

"Grant's convinced he's rocked every woman's world just by being born." Tori came off the bed and lifted her arms to the side. "I look okay? Professional?"

"Jeez, Tori," Vitto grimaced like a kid before saying good naturedly, "I'm your brother, not your fashion consultant."

Tori shot him a wry smile. "I knew our mother should've drowned you at birth. I told her you were going to be nothing but trouble."

* * * *

Quinn stared moodily at Tori. She'd come to the banquet hall on Vitto's arm and they stayed together, huddled in a corner, for most of the morning meal. He watched her from the head table and saw every soft smile and gentle nod she gave the man in what looked like an intimate moment.

Jealousy bright and hot burned inside him, causing him to slam his goblet down a little too hard. Kirill turned to him and frowned. "Is everything well, brother?"

"Fine," Quinn growled. He couldn't take it anymore. Tori was his. *Wasn't she?* He looked at her, not so sure. Suddenly, his anger was replaced by a sense of loss. He stood and stalked out of the hall. He couldn't watch the couple any longer.

* * * *

Tori watched Quinn walk out of the hall. Her eyes trailed after him long after he was gone. She wanted to follow, but held back. It was better for both of them if they didn't interact except for work.

Vitto cleared his throat to get her attention. "Tori, are you listening to me? The tissue samples from Simon should be analyzed by tonight. Grant said he was up all night with them and thinks he has the sequencing figured out. The Var have not been ruled out, but neither have six other species in our database, not to mention the species we don't know about on this planet. But, just in case, we need to compile a list of possible Var suspects and we need to figure out how we go about collecting the samples we need from them."

"What are you thinking?" Tori asked, seeing how Vitto refused to meet her direct gaze.

"Well, he was the first one to find the body," Vitto said. "It's a logical place to start."

"Quinn?" Tori breathed. "You think...?"

"I don't want to think it, but I'm first and foremost a scientist and so are you." Vitto let loose a heavy sigh. "You're worried about your actions being questioned. Well, not testing Prince Quinn as a possible suspect is one way for that to happen. I'm just telling you to cover your ass in this."

"I should've become a Galaxy Playmate like Ja ... uh, Sapphire," Tori mumbled. "We always made fun of her, but I think she was the smart one in the family sometimes. How hard could it be to take your clothes off on stage every night? Hell, she probably makes more space credits than both of us combined."

Vitto ignored the comment about their stripper sister. "All we need is a strand of the prince's hair or a mouth swab, and then we can rule him out."

"And you would like for me to get it?" Tori asked.

"You're the most likely candidate for the job. It's not like we can come out and ask for it without being insulting," Vitto said. "Though, you're the boss. If you want me to, I'll try."

"No," Tori mumbled. "If you go grabbing his hair, it will be too obvious. I'll think of something."

"Oh, crap, the king's leaving. Didn't you need to talk to him about accessing his mainframe?" Vitto pointed at the door.

"Oh, yeah. Hey, I'll find you later," Tori waved absently, as she rushed from the banquet hall to try and stop King Kirill.

* * * *

Quinn was leaning against the edge of Kirill's desk in the royal office when his brother entered. Kirill nodded at him, but didn't seem surprised to find him there.

"Have the scientists told you what they've discovered?" Kirill asked, motioning his hand to the high backed chairs before the fireplace. To the fireplace, he gently ordered, "Fire."

A fire lit, giving the room a rich orange glow. Quinn moved to a chair and took a seat. For a long time, he stared at the intricate designs on the rug near his boots. The patterns blurred before his eyes and he was forced to blink to focus them. When he only continued to stare, Kirill sighed and sat forward. Placing his hand on his knees, he angled his head to try and catch Quinn's blue eyes with his black ones.

"Have the scientists told you what they've discovered?" he repeated.

"They've found some documents in the cave systems. They're pretty old, but they think they might be able to piece them together. They didn't tell me much, but they said they'd look into them. I think they're more focused on Dr. Simon than anything else." Quinn's frown only deepened, distracted. He couldn't think, could barely bring himself to eat. His eyes turned to the tile patterns on the wall. He felt Kirill's gaze on him, but he couldn't face his brother, afraid that the king would read too many of his thoughts. Letting his gaze drift to the long banners with his family crest of an upright cat, he sighed heavily. "Though, according to Dr. Grant, they think to have found the source of black moss within the caves."

"The source?" Kirill asked. "I didn't know there was a source to it."

"Nor I. But, if you remember, some of the elders used to talk about hunting in the marshes. Now, the air is barely breathable. I think there might be something to their researching it." Quinn shrugged. He really didn't want to think about that right now, though he knew it was his duty to do just that. His mind kept wandering to Tori and Dr. Vitto. What exactly was their relationship? Friends? Lovers? One moment Quinn thought one thing, another he'd suspect something else. "Whatever it is, I doubt it's an immediate threat."

"Interesting." Kirill frowned. "I always just assumed they'd hunted the area out in the old days and the black moss overgrowth was like the green--overrun because there were no animals left to feed on it. Things were a lot less structured before our father's rule. That's Lord Myrddin's land and he's known for his fondness of hunting."

Quinn grimaced. "I know. He's not exactly the best person to try and talk with at the moment about the moss or what happened to Dr. Simon. If he knows anything about it, I doubt he'll tell us."

"He is one of the few left who won't give full support of my rule," Kirill added. "He resents that I make peace with the Draig. You don't think he had anything to do with the earth scientist's death, do you?"

"I'd like to think not," Quinn answered. "We gave our word to HIA to protect the human doctors."

"I know." Kirill frowned, sighing heavily. "I've already spoke with Franklin, at my wife's insistence, and have assured him we are helping in every way possible. It saddens me to know we failed them. I don't want the scientists going out of the palace alone."

"Agreed," Quinn answered, thinking of Tori. He'd been so scared when he couldn't find her. He never wanted to feel that way again.

"I've sent a dispatch requesting Lord Myrddin's presence at the palace, but he has yet to answer." Kirill ran his hand through his long black hair in frustration. "On one hand, he could be defying me. On the other, he could simply be away hunting."

"The biological weapons were found in his cave. Our father barely took two steps without asking him his opinion, so it's very likely he knew they existed. He could have much to hide." Quinn's look matched his brother's.

"I've thought the same thing."

"We should send Falke to invite him." Quinn's eyes again turned thoughtfully to the rug. "He can be very persuasive."

"Agreed. Let's just make sure he doesn't bring him back bound and gagged. If our suspicions are wrong...."

"I know. Lord Myrddin is a very powerful man. We can't discount him. Those who were loyal to our father are loyal still to Myrddin." Quinn felt a headache start behind one of his eyes. It was a complicated mess they faced. Reluctantly, he admitted, "I don't believe the scientists are going to be very cooperative in telling us what they've found out there in the marshes."

"After what happened to their colleague, can you blame them?" Kirill slowly stood. Looking down at Quinn, he said, "You're the ambassador. I expect you to stay close to Dr. Elliott. I want you to discover what they know."

"I'm not sure..." Quinn pushed to his feet. His weary gaze turned to Kirill and he shook his head. "I'm not sure I can. Tori ... Dr. Elliot won't see me."

"Oh?"

"I ... ah ... made her...."

"Yes?"

"Rrrr, I made her my halfmate, all right." Quinn scowled. "Only, I don't think it worked."

"How could it not work?" Kirill's lip twitched, as he tried to hide his amusement.

"I don't know. It just didn't take." Quinn shrugged and then threw his hand up in aggravation. "I probably didn't do it right. I'd never tried it before. I think our father was right about women. They drive a man to distraction if you let them."

"Ah, but it's a wonderful madness," Kirill chuckled.

"Speak for yourself. Ulyssa returns your love," Quinn grumped.

"Love?" Kirill probed, his eyes rounding in surprise.

"Ah, you know what I mean. Tor ... Dr. Elliot and I are ... were lovers only. It was a slip of the tongue." Quinn moved toward the door.

"Quinn, did Dr. Elliot know you were making her a halfmate?"

Quinn stopped and frowned. He remembered her sleepy face that last time they were together. She hadn't exactly been one hundred percent aware of what he was doing. His mouth opened to speak, but Kirill's laughter shouted out from behind.

"She didn't? Sacred Cats, little brother!" Kirill's laughter continued. "You're more hopeless than I thought!"

* * * *

"Quinn?" Tori breathed in surprise, as she nearly stumbled into his chest. She looked up. The king's rich laughter poured over them. She glanced behind his back to where Kirill stood. Slowly, she drew her gaze up. "I was just coming to speak to the king."

Quinn's face hardened, as if he would like to debate her. She narrowed her eyes in confusion. His lips tightened, his eyes hardened, as if he willed her to do something. Only, she didn't know what that something was.

When he didn't speak, merely stared, she asked lightly, "May I pass?"

Quinn suddenly stepped out of her way to let her by. She frowned in confusion, watching him storm down the long hall. What was his problem now? She shook her head, in no mood to deal with a moody prince. Turning her attention to Kirill, she watched him wave her inside.

"Your Majesty," Tori bowed her head politely, refusing to look around at the stately room. A smile twitched on his mouth at her words, as if he was amused by them. "I came to speak with you about our fallen ... about Dr. Simon's death."

Kirill's smile faded and he became serious. "You have my sincerest condolences and my word that we will do whatever we can to bring the killer to justice."

"Thank you," Tori said, doing her best to stay professional and calm. "There is actually one thing I'd like to request. We've ran some comprehensive scans that will determine the DNA of what or whoever attacked Dr. Simon. I would appreciate being allowed temporary security access to Siren's DNA database."

"You think someone from the palace did this?" Kirill asked, though he didn't seem too surprised.

"I don't know what to think. It's the most logical place to start. Your mainframe should also have records of any and all wildlife on this planet. It will help us rule that out as well."

"Done," Kirill stated. "Siren?"

"My king?" a sultry feminine voice stated, almost as if it was pouting. Tori had heard the mainframe computer speak a few times and found it amusing. Only a planet of men would make the computer's voice a seductive woman's.

"Dr. Elliot is to be allowed security clearance three into your DNA databases," Kirill said.

"New security clearance recorded, my lord," the computer purred.

Tori couldn't help but chuckle.

Kirill shrugged. "My brother, Jarek, thought it was funny to reprogram her ... *it* before he left. He placed a password on Siren's voice actuator and we haven't been able to change it back. We've all gotten used to her unique temperament."

Tori nodded.

"Just don't call her ugly. Reid did that once and it locked him in the weapons chamber for an hour until he said he was sorry." Kirill chuckled softly. Tori couldn't help but let her laugher join his.

"I'll keep that in mind," Tori answered. She bowed her head and made a move to go.

"Oh, Doctor?"

"Yes?" She turned back around.

Kirill's hand lifted to his head and he pulled out a strand of his long black hair. He offered it to her. "Here. Take this and test it. Know that you can rule me out of your suspicions."

"I did not mean to imply--"

Kirill held up a hand to stop her. "You have access to everyone but the royal family and a few of the elders. It takes more than just my word to give you clearance to that information. But, if you have a need, let me know and I will do what I can to put your mind at ease about the others. All I ask is that if you do discover something about one of my people, you talk to either my brothers or me first."

"Yes. Thank you." Tori took the hair strand and walked out of the office. The door automatically shut behind her.

"Did you get everything you needed?"

Tori glanced over at Quinn. He looked as if he'd been waiting for her. His long frame leaned against the tile wall. Lowering his jaw, his bright blue eyes bore forward to study her.

"Quinn, I don't know what you expect me to say," Tori said.

"Your face is healed," he observed. Her hand automatically lifted to touch her cheek, as she tried not to blush. "I wish to know what it is about our black moss you think to be suspicious."

Tori blinked in surprise. Work. He wanted to talk about work. All right, she could do that. "It's too early to tell, but I believe that it might be an ecological threat that is beginning to spread at a rapid pace. Already, we've discovered a mutated strand that can survive in ai ... *rah!*"

Quinn rushed forward. His hand reached to cup her face and he drew her instantly to his mouth, ending her words. Passionately, he ground his lips to hers, making her body tremble with the force of his kiss. She gasped for breath, allowing his tongue to slide inside her mouth. He massaged past her teeth, deepening the onslaught until she felt him all the way to her toes.

Just as abruptly as it started, the kiss ended. Quinn pulled back to look deep into her eyes. Tori was stunned and she gasped for breath. Her body was on fire for him, so much so that she'd been about to push his back to the wall and have her wicked way with him.

A slow smile curved on Quinn's devilishly handsome lips. "I expect a full report on the black moss situation, Dr. Elliot."

"Ah--yeah," she breathed, knowing she sounded like a simpering fool. But his kiss had been so passionate, so claiming. He'd kissed her before, but never like that, never like he was marking his territory, conquering her completely. Her lips still tingled and she could feel his tongue in her mouth as if he was still there. "Okay."

"Good," he stated with a firm nod. Tori moved to leave, clutching the king's hair strand in her fingers. "Oh, Dr. Elliot, there was one more thing."

"Yes?"

Quinn came close to her back. His breath ticked her skin, as he whispered, "You like sleeping with me. I like sleeping with you. I see no reason why we don't continue."

"But, professionalism--" she tried to interject. His hand cupped firmly to her butt, stopping her from finishing the thought. His fingers curled slightly, moving indecently close to her inner thigh. Moisture pooled within her and her head became light with pleasure. What was it about this man's nearness that sent her senses over the edge?

"If you insist, Dr. Elliot," Quinn whispered hotly, leaning forward to nip her earlobe. "What I do to this body of yours will strictly be professional."

"Ahhh," she panted, as his fingers moved to cup her sensitive flesh from behind. He rubbed a finger indecently over the length of her clothed opening. Her legs almost gave out from underneath her.

"I'll come by your suite tonight for my complete physical, doctor." With that, Quinn again nipped at her ear. Tori listened as he walked away. In a daze, she continued forward in the opposite direction, refusing to turn around to look after him.

When she reached Grant's suite, where they'd set up their new temporary laboratory, she was still stunned by Quinn's boldness. Vitto and Grant were already hard at work when she entered. Lifting her hand, she said to Grant, "Here's the king's DNA for testing. He's given me access to their database for everyone but the house nobles and royalty."

"Great," Grant said, taking the hair. He didn't bother to ask how she got it.

"What about Prince Quinn?" Vitto inquired.

"Yeah," Tori managed, before blushing. "I managed to get that too."

Vitto held out his hand for the hair strand. Tori's face turned an even deeper shade of red. "Ah, actually, you're going to need a swab for this one."

Vitto's eyes narrowed. Grant turned to her in surprise. Slowly, Tori opened her mouth.

"That's just gross, Tori! You went and gave him a blowjob? Really, that's beyond the call of duty," Grant teased.

"Ugh, Grant." Vitto flinched. "I'm pretending I didn't hear that!"

"Saliva sample, moron," Tori returned. She looked at Vitto, who grabbed a swab and merely shook his head.

"What lengths you'll go to in the name of science," Grant chuckled, moving to begin sequencing on the king's hair.

Chapter Eight

Tori spent all day working in the laboratory, but for once, she didn't forget about the time. She was actually anticipating finishing up for the night. Just the thought of Quinn made her shake with anticipation to be near him. Usually she was all about the work, even though trying to figure out who killed Dr. Simon was a grim task.

Rubbing her neck, she leaned back in her chair, turning away from the computer screen floating before her. She'd been staring at if for hours, waiting for it to complete its analysis. The computer was sequencing the DNA and all she could was pray that it turned out to be a wild animal.

"Anything yet?" Vitto asked.

"No," Tori answered, yawning.

The computer beeped, signaling that it was finished. Both of them jumped and Grant came rushing across the room holding three cups of coffee. Absently, he set them down on the table.

"Was it an animal?" Grant asked, almost hopeful.

Tori paled, slowly shaking her head in denial. She stared at the screen, unable to speak. Her hand came to rest over her mouth.

"No," Vitto answered. He glanced at his sister, before slashing his hand through the nearly transparent screen in agitation. When he'd finished, the screen went back to normal. "He was killed by a Var."

All three scientists stared at the information before them. Finally, steeling herself, Tori said, "Siren, I need DNA access. Please match our computer's sequencing with Var DNA samples in your database."

"Yes, Dr. Elliot," the computer's sultry voice answered, its purring out of place in the solemn room. "Match sequencing begun. Estimated time six hours and forty-three minutes."

"I'll take the couch," Vitto said, automatically knowing none of them would want to leave until the palace's mainframe had finished its comparisons. "We might as well try to get some rest while we're waiting."

"Elliot, why don't you take the bed?" Grant offered. "I'll lie on the floor."

"No, why don't you take the couch? Vitto and I can share the bed." Tori sighed. The men nodded in agreement. It was going to be a long night and they had nothing to do but wait.

* * * *

Quinn paced back and forth in Tori's suite, waiting for her to join him. He'd brought more flowers, which were getting harder to find. Taura had guards on her garden now, so he had to find the pretty weeds elsewhere. He stopped, chuckling like an ill-behaved boy who'd gotten away with mischief as he thought about it.

Taura was beside herself with irritation, though the noblewoman would hardly let it show. If she found out it was him, she'd probably try to put him in isolation as punishment, locking him in his room for three days without company--as she'd done to the princes as young boys. The very idea of a fifty-six year old man getting sent to his room was hilarious.

Throwing himself down on the couch, he stared at the ceiling. He could tell by the light that it was getting late. Quinn frowned. His leg restlessly swung over the side of the couch, kicking into the air with agitation. Where was she anyway? He'd been pacing anxiously for hours, counting down the slow minutes until he could be with her again.

After a half hour on the couch, he slowly pushed himself up. His hands pulled at his light brown hair. He hated to admit it, but it looked like she wasn't going to come.

"Fire," he stated, angry. The fire lit in the fireplace. Going across to his flowers, he grabbed them and threw them into the flames.

* * * *

Tori yawned, blinking heavily. She lay on Grant's bed by her brother. The room was dark, the top dome curtains drawn overhead to cast the whole suite into blackness. She felt the bed shift next to her and assumed Vitto tossed in his sleep. She couldn't blame him. She felt the same way-- restless, edgy.

Sadness overwhelmed her for a moment as she thought of Simon. He'd been such a decent man, a respected colleague, a good friend. She still hadn't been able to bring herself to go through his belongings. It somehow seemed wrong to invade his personal things.

The bed shifted again. Tori closed her eyes, tired, as she tried to get some more sleep. She flipped over on her side.

"Snookie, you in here?"

Tori was so exhausted, it took her a moment to realize someone had spoken. She frowned, wondering if she was dreaming. Reluctantly, she opened her eyes.

"Snookie, where are you? I've come to play." It was a woman's voice.

Suddenly, a hand was on the coverlet over her leg, inching up to her thigh. A giggle sounded, jolting her to complete awareness. Tori shot up in bed, gasping. Her leg shot out, trying to get away from the caress. She ended up kicking Vitto in the side. He grunted and there was a tumbling of arms and legs on the bed.

It was dark and she couldn't see anything. The woman screamed. Tori was smacked in the face by a flying arm. She lifted her hands to block her face and ended up elbowing Vitto in the stomach. The irritating woman screamed again--high pitched and loud.

"What the...?" Grant's voice drifted over them, sleepily. There was a noise as he stumbled about in the dark.

The woman shifted her weight and Tori fell over on her side, her head hitting Vitto's leg. She could barely move, as the coverlet twisted around her. The woman's head fell on her stomach, trapping her even more.

"Lights!"

Tori froze, gasping for breath. Quinn's voice rang over the suite. The curtains were pulled around the dome. She blinked as a soft, diffused light flooded over them.

Her body was pinned between Vitto and Linzi. Linzi was naked, except for a robe. Tori flinched, trying to buck the woman off. Linzi screamed again, seeing that she was in the bed with the wrong people. Tori glared at Grant to shut the woman up. She couldn't see Quinn, but she felt his presence.

Grant snickered in amusement, as he crossed over to the bed. He yanked Linzi's arm and pulled her upright. She glared at him, then at the bed, before storming out of the room.

Tori wiggled around to see Quinn. His face was red with anger. He glared at Vitto. As she stared up at him, his eyes turned to her. His lip curled up in a snarl. Without saying a word, he turned and stormed from the suite.

"What the hell was that?" Grant asked.

"Help me out of this," Tori demanded, torn as to whether or not she should chase Quinn.

"Sequencing complete," Siren announced overhead, making her mind up for her. All three scientists froze.

Vitto sprung into action, untangling their limbs. Standing, Tori gasped for breath and asked, "Siren, was there a match?"

"No match within my database," Siren answered.

"Thank you, Siren," Tori said, remembering what the king had said about the computer being temperamental.

"You're welcome, Dr. Elliot."

"What about King Kirill? Prince Quinn?" Tori asked.

"It's not them," Grant said. "They have a common thread that must have come from their father. I'm guessing it's none of the princes."

"That leaves the elders, Lord Myrddin to be exact." Tori frowned, letting her professional calm overtake her. They'd discussed the possibility of him before. It was his land the biological weapons were on. His cave was the source of the black moss. Plus, Quinn mentioned he didn't support Kirill's rule. It only made sense.

"Often the easiest, most logical choice is the right one," Vitto said.

Tori nodded. "You're right. I think it's time I met this Lord Myrddin for myself."

* * * *

"No."

Tori stared at Quinn in disbelief. After going back to her suite to take a quick bath, she searched the castle for him. Finally getting directions to his wing of the palace from one of the guards, she went to the hall where she'd first met him--lips locked to Linzi.

Quinn's home was simple in its taste, colored with rich blues and cream. A couch sat before a large fireplace on a slightly raised platform. The couch was low and wide. Long pillows were laid out on the floor, perfect for lounging. The wide tiled floor stretched before the front door, elegant and immaculately clean.

Aside from the front, there were no doors in the prince's home. Tall decorative arches in the wall led to a bedroom, a kitchen, and a large office. A wall of glass, so thick you couldn't see through it, guarded the bathroom. An inlet next to the fireplace, near the kitchen, led to a large dining room. There were enough chairs in it to seat more than a dozen guests.

"It's beautiful," Tori had said in awe upon entering, her eyes wide.

"What do you want, Dr. Elliot?" was Quinn's cold reply.

Now, staring at his dispassionate face, she stiffened. Looking at him was like looking at a stranger. There was no affection in him, no tenderness or teasing. He was all ambassador, and it stung her to the core. Any impulse she had to explain the morning fiasco was swallowed up inside.

"What do you mean no?" Tori demanded, placing her hands on her hips.

"I've read your file. You have several degrees, Dr. Elliot. I assume you know the meaning of the word. The answer to your request is no." Quinn studied her, his bright blue eyes burning hotly from his blank face. She shivered. "I won't take you to Lord Myrddin, especially without knowing why you need to meet him."

"Quinn," she began, wanting to explain. His brow rose. Rubbing her temples, she shook her head. "I'll file my preliminary findings with the king. Good day."

Tori turned and walked out the front door. Her shoulder's jerked, but she refused to cry. She had to be strong.

Quinn watched the door close behind her. His hand reached forward to go after her, but he pulled it back to his side. In the brief moment she said his name, her eyes had been defeated, sad, exhausted beyond measure. He wanted to comfort her, to hold her. However, the memory of her on the bed with Vitto and Linzi wouldn't leave him. Later, after he calmed down, he realized he didn't know what they were doing, or if they were doing anything at all. But, it had taken him a long time to calm himself to that point.

Quinn took a deep breath. His sudden jealousy over it was too potent to ignore. He'd been mindless with rage and that wasn't a good sign. It meant he was starting to feel more than just a passing connection to her. He couldn't afford distractions in his life, not to the extent that he couldn't function. His father's incessant words came back to him. *"This kingdom is what makes us, Quinn, this land. A man cannot bow to a woman and still call himself a man. To fall for a woman is to fall for weakness. We are men. We conquer and rule. We must be strong and, as ambassador, you must be the strongest of mind. If you allow yourself to ever be distracted, your folly could be the death of our race. Remember that, the next time some pretty thing turns your head. If ever your heart begins to beat a woman's name, think of the Var race rotting in the sun in a sea of corpses. That is what love can do, my son. Take your pleasure, enjoy their soft company, but never get attached. Duty must always come first."*

Closing his eyes, he could still see his father's serious face as he said the words to a young prince who would help lead a nation. Afterwards, King Attor had smiled at him, a rare expression on the old king. *"Besides, women are like fruit on the vine, each piece sweeter than the first. Why sample one, when you can sample them all?"*

Quinn turned and forced himself to go back to the tall stack of papers in his office awaiting his attention. He was smart enough to understand that his father didn't know everything. Hell, Attor had been wrong when he had the biological weapons brought to the planet. The man was no saint. But, for all his faults, King Attor had been wise. His logic in many things could not be discounted.

Kirill had found happiness with his wife, but could Quinn hope to ever have the same? Shaking his head, he highly doubted it. Ulyssa clearly returned her husband's love. Dr. Elliot, however, barely appeared to give him a second thought unless he was standing in front of her, blatantly demanding attention with sexual overtures. No, falling for the scientist wasn't a safe bet and a man in his royal position couldn't afford to gamble.

* * * *

Tori gripped her report in her hand, crumpling and twisting it, as she nervously waited for the door to the king's office to open. She'd spent the entire morning writing the thing and still wasn't satisfied with it. Her mind was too distracted to focus on anything but Quinn. The only reason she wrote the thing to begin with was because she'd told Quinn that she would. He'd just frustrated her so much when she went to his home. Well, if he wanted to act professional, she could act professional.

"King Kirill," Tori nodded her head, stepping into his office.

"Ah, Doctor," the king said, standing up from his desk. He smiled kindly at her.

Tori nodded, stiffly trying to return the friendly gesture.

"Dr. Elliot, I don't believe we've really had a chance to properly meet."

At the statement, Tori turned to Queen Ulyssa. The queen was a beautiful woman, one who looked incredibly happy. Even when she wasn't smiling, the love shone from her eyes.

"Majesty," Tori said.

Ulyssa laughed. "Oh, not you, too! Please, call me Ulyssa. I still haven't been able to get used to this 'Your Royal Highness' business. But, at least you didn't curtsey. That's something at least."

Chuckling, Tori couldn't seem to help herself. Ulyssa's expression was too open and friendly.

"So, how do you like working for HIA?" Ulyssa asked, laughing at her own private joke.

"It's...."

"I know," Ulyssa put forth when Tori hesitated. "They don't give you much choice, do they?"

Tori glanced at the king and then back to Ulyssa. "No, not really."

"I was sorry to hear about Dr. Simon. He was a nice man." The queen crossed over and laid a gentle hand on her arm. Tori nodded, her expression fading into a blank mask. Her attention was again drawn to the report clutched in her hand. Leaning forward, Ulyssa whispered in her ear, under the pretense of giving her a hug, "These Var men are a handful, but I promise their brains do eventually catch up to their hearts. I know it's frustrating, but try to have patience. And, if that doesn't work, be blunt or hit Quinn over the head until he sees reason or blacks out." The queen pulled back and winked. "Either way, I guarantee it will make you feel better. Quinn's a good man and he'll be honest with you, if ever you have a need to demand the truth from him."

Tori wasn't sure what to say to that. Did everyone assume that since she and Quinn were lovers there was more to their relationship? She did care for him, and his dismissal earlier had hurt a great deal. Smiling politely, she nodded as the queen pulled completely away.

"I'm here if you need to talk," Ulyssa said. She crossed over to her husband and, without embarrassment, wrapped her arms around his neck. He leaned down, returning her light embrace as he gave her a gentle kiss. Pulling away, she said, "I'll see you in an hour. Don't make me come back here and force you to eat. It won't be pretty if you forget again."

"Yes, dear," he laughed, not looking at all threatened.

Tori averted her eyes at the loving interplay. Ulyssa touched her shoulder as she walked past, leaving her alone with King Kirill.

"I prepared a report on our findings," Tori announced. She stepped to the desk and held out the papers. Kirill glanced at it and slowly took it, before setting it on his desk unopened.

"It wasn't necessary for you to go to all this trouble," Kirill said. "Oral reports are fine."

"You'll find on page three the DNA evidence we were able to salvage from Dr. Simon," Tori said.

"I can tell by your tone that you suspect one of my people," Kirill returned, his voice quiet. An extreme sadness crossed over his features. "For that I am sorry. Why don't you tell me what you know?"

Tori took a deep breath. Following Kirill to the chairs set before the fireplace, she sat down. It took a moment for her to speak. Then, looking at his concerned face, she told him everything she'd discovered.

When she was finished, the king said, "I hate to admit it, but I agree that Lord Myrddin is the most logical choice. The news about the black moss is disturbing to say the least. Do you think you can help us stop it?"

Tori nodded. "I believe we can, given enough time. If we know exactly what the black moss is and how and why it was created, that would really speed up the process. It's imperative I speak with Lord Myrddin. Not only do I need a DNA sample to rule him out, but I need to know what exactly they were doing in that cave. The records we took were too corrupted by time to translate into any kind of recognizable data."

"Prince Falke and Prince Reid are going to Lord Myrddin's home. They leave tomorrow. You may accompany them if you wish." Kirill stood and moved to place his hand on her shoulder. "I want you to heed their advice while you're gone. Actually, I insist upon it. They know Lord Myrddin and they know the marshes."

"Thank you. We will." Tori stood. Kirill's hand fell from her arm. "Please let Prince Falke know that we'll be ready to leave at first light."

* * * *

Quinn stormed into his brother's office, scowling as he demanded, "What do you mean she can go? Are you insane?"

Kirill had the audacity to grin at him. "I wondered how long it would take you to find out."

"It's too dangerous," Quinn put forth, ignoring his brother's teasing. "Would you send Ulyssa?"

"Ah, you see, Ulyssa is my mate. Dr. Elliot is a scientist who means nothing to us, except on a professional basis. Isn't that what you said earlier?" Kirill's grin widen as Quinn's expression hardened and turned red. "Besides, with Ulyssa I wouldn't allow anything, she'd just do it. I can't stop her from being who she is. It's one of the reasons I love her."

Quinn began to curse, a long string of words in their native tongue.

"Feel better?" Kirill asked with he'd finished.

"No," Quinn grumbled. "If that foolish woman insists on this madness and you are too ignorant to stop her, then I must go with them."

Kirill's mouth opened. Before he could speak, Quinn growled.

"I'm not asking for your permission, brother," Quinn stated. "I'm going with them."

Kirill didn't move. Turning on his heel, Quinn left the office the same way he came.

Chapter Nine

Tori stretched her arms over her head and yawned. Everything the three scientists needed for the trip was packed. They weren't bringing much, except for some basic instruments and their personal belongings. Looking at Vitto, she opened her mouth to speak. Before she uttered a syllable, the door to Grant's suite swung open.

"Quinn...?" she began, moving to stand up. His face was red with anger and she knew he'd found out about her plans to confront Lord Myrddin. Trembling, she took a step back.

Quinn stormed forward to grab her. Vitto came forward to block his path. The prince looked at him, his eyes shifting dangerously as he growled in warning.

"Vitto, no, it's all right," Tori said, not wanting to see her brother hurt. "I know what this is about."

"Come on," Quinn growled. He grabbed her arm and forcibly pulled her out the door. Dragging her down the long halls, he didn't speak.

"Quinn, what are you doing?" Tori demanded, trying to pull her arm free as she tripped to keep up with his swift pace. "Let me go! You're hurting my arm."

They came to the hall before his home and he stopped. Turning to her, he dropped her arm. His eyes dared her to try and run. Tori didn't move, sensing that he would surely catch her if she tried to escape. She shivered, seeing how close he was to shifting. Claws were drawn on his fingers. Looking at her shoulder, she tensed. They'd ripped through her lab coat and ESC jumpsuit.

"Quinn? What's going on with you?" Her words were a whisper, shaking slightly in light of his outrage. "You're not the same as when I met you. Are you ... sick? You don't seem well. I'm a doctor, granted not that kind of doctor, but I can help you. Are you sick?"

"I told you no," he stated, ignoring her questions. "It's not safe for you to go to Lord Myrddin's. I don't want you going. Let Grant and Vitto do it."

"That's not your decision to make. It's mine. Besides, it's my job to go." Tori took a calming breath, trying to sound reasonable. "I owe it to Simon to uncover the truth. Furthermore, I started a job on this planet and I intend to finish it. I'm the one in charge and I refuse to hide like a coward just because I'm scared."

"It's my duty to protect you!" Quinn growled in frustration. His chest heaved. "How can I protect you if you don't listen to me?"

The comment struck Tori as odd. She swallowed, nervous. "Why is it your duty? Because I'm a scientist and you the Var ambassador?"

Quinn's expression hardened at her words and his eyes darted away. He hesitated, before stating, "Yes, that's why. It's my responsibility to make sure what happened to Dr. Simon doesn't happen to the rest of you. If you truly believe Lord Myrddin is the killer, then it's not safe for you to confront him. You're human. He's a Var warrior. He'll be able to kill you with one swipe of his claw and you won't even see it coming."

"Your concern is noted," Tori answered, hardening her look to match his. "Prince Reid and Prince Falke will be escorting us. I have no doubts they will provide adequate protection for myself and my team. If you're concerned about political backlash from HIA should something happen, I'll be happy to sign a waver."

"I'm coming, too," Quinn answered. His jaw flexed. His bright blue eyes were rigid with anger. She was sorry to see the playful expression he usually carried was completely gone.

Tori glanced down, seeing his claws hadn't retracted. He might be hiding it better, but he was still very angry. Unable to answer, she merely nodded. She was surprised by his admission, though she knew she shouldn't be.

"You will obey my orders while we are gone," Quinn continued, working back into his rampage. His voice rose, dictating as he said, "This is not negotiable."

Tori bit her lip and lowered her voice as she stepped closer to him. Very clearly, she answered, "I will tell you what I will do while we are gone, Prince Quinn. I *will* question Lord Myrddin about Dr. Simon. I *will* clear Qurilixen of biological weaponry. I *will* find a way to stop the black moss from continuing to spread. Do you realize in anywhere from ten to thirty years your whole planet could be dead from it? Now, if in doing these three very important things I happen to obey your will for me, then great. But, if your will jeopardizes my ability to do my job, then ... ahh!"

Tori gasped as Quinn shot forward. She flinched, thinking he meant to strike. Instead, he grabbed her face and yanked her body to his. His lips found hers in a bruising kiss that both punished and rewarded. His fingers thrust back into her hair, giving her no choice of escape. She felt the tips of claws scraping dangerously close to her scalp, but they didn't hurt her.

Passion built within her at his display of strength. His hold had never been so dominating. He was always confident, but usually his touch was worshipping, not demanding. His head shifted, slanting his mouth hard to hers, punishing her lips as he thrust his tongue deep inside her mouth.

Heat curled in her stomach, rolling over her until she couldn't think. Primal animal instinct overtook them as Tori moaned. Her hands reached to pull his tight body closer. The feel of his arousal burned into her. Her mouth moved, meeting his demands with some of her own.

Before she realized what was happening, he had her pressed up against the hallway wall, trapped beneath his searching hands. His fingers were everywhere, her breasts, her thighs, her waist, her back. He broke his lips from hers only to trail to her neck to place hot, sucking kisses over her throat. His tongue drew over her flesh, tasting her.

"Ahh!" Tori gasped, clutching to him. The hard stone of the tile wall was unforgiving against her back, but not as much as the man before her. She heard a rip and felt her jumpsuit parting down the front. His claw snagged the material, opening it all the way to her thighs. The heat of his chest soaked into her breasts as he leaned into her, making her nipples incredibly hard.

His hands left her, but she still couldn't move because the full press of his length kept her pinned. She felt his weight shift. Quinn's mouth found her earlobe and he bit passionately at it before rimming her ear with his tongue. When his weight shifted again and his hands returned to push apart the torn pieces of her jumpsuit, she felt his heavy arousal against her thigh.

"Quinn," she said breathlessly. Vaguely she was aware that they were in the hallway, where anyone could walk by.

His answer was a throaty, dark, possessive growl. Fingers cupped her large breasts, massaging them in feverish circles, pinching the buds until they screamed for more. Next, his hands moved to her hips, jerking her up against the wall. He expertly angled his hips between her thighs. She had no choice but to let her legs fall open. In one swift movement, he embedded himself deep, sliding in the cream of her body's excitement.

"Mine," Quinn growled, over and over, low and dark. His eyes held hints of green within their blue depths. "Mine."

Tori couldn't understand his words, as he spoke in his own growling language. She trembled violently. He began to move, slipping in and out of her, building a sweet ache deep within her core. His rhythm was fast and hard, ferociously claiming her like a wild beast.

Suddenly, she climaxed so hard her teeth chattered and all she could do was moan and pant insensibly. Her body clamped down on him, spasming so fiercely that he had no choice but to find his own release. It came to him with shaking force, racking their bodies together.

His hands weakened and he let her slide down to the floor. Their breaths mingled, coming harshly from their parted lips. Quinn forehead fell against hers. Her eyes lifted to his. He was so close she could feel every inch of him. The pupils in his eyes dilated.

"You will obey my orders while we are gone," Quinn whispered, repeating his earlier decree. "This is not negotiable."

Tori gasped. Quinn spun around on his heels, leaving her in the hall as he stormed into his home, slamming the door behind him.

Tori stared for a long moment, wondering if what had just happened was meant to be a punishment. She didn't feel punished at all. She'd felt his desire for her, taken out in the frustration of his body's thrusts. Then, glancing down, she saw her naked body, exposed by the torn jumpsuit. Quickly, she pulled her lab coat together and took off down the hall for her suite.

* * * *

Prince Falke was ready to leave the palace at dawn. Siren was called upon to awaken the scientists. Unfortunately for the stoic commander, and the roused scientists, Prince Reid didn't stumble into the banquet hall until almost noon. Tori knew that Reid lived outside the palace, in the forest, near the Draig border, so it was unlikely Siren could give him the same wake up call she'd given the others.

Most of the morning, Quinn, Kirill, and Falke talked amongst themselves at one of the tables. Servants brought around drinks. The scientists formed their own group two tables away, going over paperwork and strategies for handling Lord Myrddin.

Tori did her best not to look at the handsome Quinn. He hadn't spoken to her since their encounter in the hall. He barely even acknowledged her. His dismissal hurt deeply, causing a low ache in her chest. She swallowed the pain and concentrated on work. Tori never expected their relationship to last forever, but neither was she ready for it to end. Thankfully, Vitto and Grant had the good sense not to ask her about it.

Since her black jumpsuit was now torn, Tori wore the clothing of the Var. She pulled the laces tight at her hips, closing the material all the way. The pants molded to her like a second skin, but she was happy that her outer thighs didn't peak through the side laces. The sleeveless shirt was perfect for the warmer weather. It hugged just as tight around her breasts. Her sides were exposed, but she pretended not to care. The truth was, she felt damned sexy in the outfit and was disappointed Quinn hadn't noticed.

When Reid finally walked in, he merely winked at his brothers, giving them a sheepish grin. He was dark featured and moved with the steady grace of his brothers. Muscles formed his body and he carried them proudly, as if he expected women to swoon at his feet. Falke didn't comment, just grunted as he rose to depart. They all followed suit, slinging backpacks over their shoulders as they prepared for the hike.

As they neared the side gate to the palace, Quinn dropped back and fell into step next to Tori. She blinked, looking at him in surprise. He glanced at her, his blank face giving nothing away, as he said, "I've been assigned to your protection. Falke will look after Grant. Reid will look after Vitto."

Tori looked ahead and saw that each prince fell into stride with the other two men. They went straight into the forest, going to the shadowed marshes. Tightly, she stated, "We can take care of ourselves. We don't need to be looked after like children."

The words were soft. For a long moment Quinn acted as if he hadn't heard her. She was about to repeat herself when he finally answered. "It is the king's wish that it be so. We will not risk your lives while you remain under our protection. Resign yourself to it, Dr. Elliot, or we will be forced to turn back around."

Tori refused to answer. The idea of Quinn protecting her was oddly comforting, even though he didn't appear too pleased with the task. She really wasn't trained for physical combat. Now a verbal debate was something she could win.

They continued to walk in silence for a few hours. Falke set a rigid pace, but none complained. Tori was too preoccupied to notice. Quinn stayed close, but his eyes didn't turn to her, he didn't smile, and he didn't talk. Ahead of them Reid laughed and joked good-naturedly with Grant and Vitto. Leading the group was Falke by himself.

"When will we arrive?" Tori asked. It was very warm and sweat had begun to bead on her flesh, making her clothes stick.

"At this pace? Tomorrow." Quinn finally looked down at her. He'd been doing his best to convince himself that he didn't care for her, that he only wanted her as a lover, a diversion. He was afraid it wasn't working.

The silence was killing him inside, but he refused to end it. They came from different worlds. When the job was over, she'd be leaving him behind. Qurilixen was his home and he wouldn't be running out on it like his brother Jarek. It was his duty to stay, his destiny, and his choice. He was content in his life, or at least he had been until he met Dr. Tori Elliot.

"So we camp?" she asked.

Quinn glanced down to her. Sacred Cats! She was beautiful in his native clothing. He'd been stunned when he saw her in the outfit. He wondered if she knew that the effect the tightened laces had on her backside, pulling the material tight across her butt. He nearly groaned to remember it and had an insane urge to fall behind just to get another glimpse.

"Yes," he answered, a little too late.

Damn, but he couldn't concentrate around her. He knew he sounded harsh, but after spending the entire journey walking so close to her intoxicating scent, he was about to go mad with lust. The encounter in the palace hall only fueled his desire for her. He hadn't meant to take her like that but, when she didn't protest, he couldn't stop himself. Afterwards, alone in his home, he'd been confounded by his total lack of control.

"Hey, Tori!" Vitto called. His smiling face turned around amidst a round of laughter. He waved at her to join them. "Tori, come here, you have to hear these stories!"

Tori spared a brief glance at Quinn, before hiking forward to join the men. Grant was laughing so hard that tears formed in the corners of his eyes. Vitto grinned. Reid was chuckling, but a moment's worry passed over his face as she joined them.

"Ah, go ahead," Grant said, still laughing. "Elliot here's just like a man, aren't you Elliot?"

"Yes," she drawled, "just."

Reid's gaze narrowed, as he blatantly checked her out. His eyes stopped a second too long on her breasts and a smile of male appreciation crossed over his lips. When he looked back up at her, his eyes danced with amusement. His brow rose and Tori had the distinct impression the look of masculine invitation was meant to aggravate Quinn more than entice her. In a low, flirtatious tone, he murmured, "She looks very much a woman to me."

Tori blushed, knowing he said it loud enough so Quinn could hear him. Hearing a noise, they all turned to see Quinn righting himself from the ground. He'd tripped. His eyes met Tori's and he wasn't smiling.

"Watch out for the path, brother," Reid taunted. "It has a tendency to jump out at you."

Vitto and Grant snickered, but hid their expression.

"It's not the path, brother," Quinn returned. "It's the back of your ugly head."

"I'll have you know women find my head particularly attractive," Reid returned, not at all insulted. Keeping a straight face, he added flippantly, "As well as the rest of me."

Tori couldn't help it. She laughed outright at his conceit. Reid was so full of himself, and yet seemed not to take himself seriously at all. Quinn grumbled behind them. Reid's smile only widened.

"All right, my lady," Reid said gallantly.

"Back off Reid," Falke called, his voice full of warning. "I don't want to have to dunk you in the swamp."

"Ah, you stay out of it!" Reid answered good-naturedly. Tori blinked in confusion and finally concluded it must be a private joke between brothers. "This is between Dr. Elliot and me. I can't help it if she's attracted to me."

Tori's mouth fell open at the audacity. In truth, she thought Reid was funny. He was handsome, but she could only think of the moody prince walking behind them. Reid turned to her and winked. To her amazement, she blushed again.

"Stop flirting with Elliot and tell us another story," Grant interjected.

Tori stared straight ahead.

"Oh, let me see," Reid began, humming softly in thought. "When Falke was, oh, twenty four or thereabouts, he was already in charge of the soldiers and, being his younger brothers, Jarek, Quinn, and I had to train under him. Well, we'd been at blades for about a week when Quinn decided it would be a good idea to skip practice. Now, understand that Falke was a real taskmaster and didn't take kindly to us not showing up. When he told our father, which in hindsight he was duty bound to do, the king locked us in the dungeon for a week without food."

Tori grimaced. She didn't have too high of an opinion of King Attor to begin with, but to hear he'd lock someone up for a week without food just for being young and obnoxious? It was a little extreme. How hard it must've been for them, growing up with such an emotionally distant man as a father. She'd been very lucky. Her parents were both good people who gave all their children lots of love and encouragement. Vitto and Grant didn't seem all that affected by the fact, so she left it alone.

"Naturally, we tired to escape," Reid continued, chuckling. "Quinn, being the smallest, was ... um ... volunteered for the job and--"

"It was your idea to skip," Quinn stated from behind, his voice not as hard as before. Reid sighed dramatically at being interrupted. "And, if I remember correctly, you two volunteered me by shoving me through the dungeon bars against my will."

"We'd thought you'd fit," Reid answered, shrugging. "How were we to know you'd get stuck?"

"I don't know, logic?" Quinn returned, chuckling slightly. Tori glanced back at him, catching a glimpse of the easygoing prince she'd first met. Her heart skipped to see the soft, kind expression on his face. What had happened to make him so hard lately?

"Ah, logic is overrated," Reid waved him back. "You were only there for three days so stop being a baby."

"You threw rocks at my ass the entire time," Quinn returned. Vitto and Grant laughed. Tori's mind was still stuck on the fact that they weren't fed for a week.

"We were bored." Reid moved closer to Tori and said, "Just picture, Quinn's scrawny little butt hanging out of the bars. You'd have thrown rocks at it too."

Tori chuckled, more at Reid's facial expression than his story. Reid turned his attention forward as the path narrowed. He gallantly gestured Tori to go ahead of him.

Quinn watched in irritation as Tori's soft laughter rang through the forest. He wished it had been he who put the look on her beautiful face. He frowned at his brother. Reid's head was tilted to the side and it wasn't hard to see that he was staring at Tori's tight pants. Quinn took the opportunity to lay a hand on Reid's shoulder, gripping into it tightly.

"Watch yourself, brother," he warned, before backing away once more.

Chapter Ten

"I've seen your look before," Reid said, coming to sit beside Quinn on the ground. He sighed, looking over the campsite. There was a small fire and a couple basic tents. The sky was softening to a light haze of green. The three scientists talked privately amongst themselves, debating some paper they'd brought with them.

Quinn glanced at Reid and sighed, not wanting to hear it. He knew where his brother was going with this. He loved Reid, but right now he was irritated with him.

Reid had spent the entire day being his fabulously charming self, telling stories, drawing attention--something the man did naturally. Though serious about his work, he had a careless, fun air to him that drew women better than a magical love charm. And he had a predilection for bedding many women--sometimes at the same time--and didn't care who knew it. That Reid didn't understand the love of one woman didn't surprise Quinn at all.

"I've seen it on Kirill when he looks at Ulyssa." There was a pause as Reid looked over at Tori. A slight frown crossed his features. "I don't want to see you fall into the same trap. One brother life mated is bad enough, but two? It will look as if we don't have the prowess to handle many women in our beds. Beyond that, you are my brother and I worry. You can't take life mating back once it's done. Surely, you'd grow tired bedding the same woman all the time."

"Who said anything about life mating? As soon as this whole mess is over, she's gone. End of story. Leave me be about it." Quinn reached down, flipping over a rock only to watch the black moss turn grey in the air. He'd never really stopped to contemplate the moss at all before Tori pointed it out. They'd grown up with it. Now he wondered if there really was something to what she said about it slowly killing off his planet.

"Just be careful, brother," Reid put forth. "You must not allow yourself to become deluded by good sex. So what if she's good in bed? It doesn't mean there isn't someone better waiting to take her place. And if not better, at least different. You remember what our father said about variety? Without it, a man grows frustrated and bored. With frustration come mistakes in judgment. It's all the more reason not to bind yourself to her."

"I'm not binding myself to anyone. Besides, don't tell me what to do," Quinn responded, a bit harshly. "I certainly don't need you quoting our father to me. I know no one is saying it, but we all know this mess we're in right now is his fault. Where was his infinite wisdom when he risked our people's lives by bringing that damned weapon here? Sacred Cats! If the people knew the whole truth, they'd probably revolt and kill us all. If you seek to make a point to me, you'd best not do it by using King Attor's wisdom! Anyway, my personal life is none of your concern."

"What is happening to this family? First Kirill, now you? Do you honestly think the small reward of having only one woman beats the weakness to be gained by it?" Reid ran a frustrated hand through his hair. "Don't get me wrong. I like our new queen just fine and I like Dr. Elliot. But, why not halfmate them and take other wives? I don't understand."

"You seemed to understand my attraction well enough when you were flirting with her," Quinn grumbled.

"I was testing her, proving a point. She'll not be loyal to you. She's a liability," Reid answered. "I'm not blind. I see how she ignores you for those human males. You didn't speak two words to each other on the hike today."

"I don't want nor need her to be tested." Quinn's eyes turned red with his anger. "Especially by you."

"What?" Reid taunted. Neither of them had moved from their place on the ground. "Afraid she'd fail? Afraid I'd be able to woo her to my bed easily enough?"

Quinn gulped and couldn't speak. Standing, he turned to glance at Tori. Her attention was turned to Vitto and they were whispering. They did indeed look cozy, sitting together on the fallen log. "I'll be back. I'm going for a walk."

"A walk?" Reid repeated. "But, we just stopped walking."

Quinn ignored him, storming off into the forest. He didn't want to hear Reid's damned logic. He just wanted his life to go back to the way it was, before Tori Elliot stumbled into it. He wanted to laugh and feel carefree again. Growling, he began to jog. He really needed to get away from her. That earth scientist was likely to drive him mad.

* * * *

Tori sighed, enjoying the cool trickling waterfall spilling over her shoulders. The small pool was carved into the smooth, red tinted rock, which kept it from getting contaminated by the surrounding swampland. Just to be sure, they tested it before she got in.

The day was so warm and, after hiking for several hours, her clothes had stuck uncomfortably to her skin. Turning, she let the water hit over her breasts. She was about as clean as she was going to get, but she couldn't bring herself to get out. Her head tipped back, as she thought of what she was doing on the strange planet.

To her surprise, she found her relationship with Quinn stressed her out more than her duty as a scientist. Just thinking about him made her heart ache and there was nothing she could do to make it stop. She couldn't run tests, make charts, and develop theories. For in the end one thing remained constant--she didn't know what Quinn was thinking.

Tori hated uncertainty. It's one of the reasons she liked being a scientist. She liked having a plan of action. She liked finding a solution to a problem. But, in all her life, she'd never faced a problem like she did now. Part of her said that it didn't matter at all what she did or felt, and that she would soon be leaving Qurilixen and Quinn behind for good.

Hearing a splash near the rocky shore, she turned in surprise. Quinn came at her, walking through the shallow pool to where she stood. He still wore his clothes. They stuck seductively to his skin where the water splashed up on him.

Tori tried to cover her breasts, as she said, "Quinn, what are you doing here? Someone might see us."

"We need to talk," he answered. His face was hard, not giving anything away as he came to stand before her. The breeze blew his untamed hair over his shoulders. His bright blue eyes blazed with a hint of liquid gold-green. He looked fierce, wild. Her heart fluttered in her chest and her knees nearly weakened out from beneath her.

"About what?" Tori asked, breathless. A buzz sounded in her ears, making her feel faint. Her body remembered their last joining in the hall of the palace. She'd never done anything as dangerous as being with him in public. It thrilled her. She wanted to do it again. Her eyes dipped down over his solid frame. The breeze hugged his shirt to his back, whipping it back and forth over his firm stomach.

"Us."

She shivered. The admission didn't seem to bring him much pleasure. It could only mean one thing. He was going to break it off completely. Tori didn't move. Whispering, she asked weakly, "What about us?"

"How do you do it?" he demanded, his expression becoming almost desperate.

"What do I do?" Tori leaned back, unsure what was wrong with him. His eyes filled with green and the pupils elongated slightly. She panted--excited, fearful, aroused.

"I'm trying to understand," he admitted, his voice low and soft. His eyes narrowed and moved down her neck to her covered breasts, as if seeing them for the first time. For a moment, he stared at them like a man starved.

"What did I do?" Tori asked again, heated by his possessive gaze on her body. She felt very exposed standing naked before him.

"You don't trust me at all, do you, Tori?" he answered at length. His hand reached as if he would touch her, but then fell back.

"What are you talking about?" Tori trembled. "I don't understand what is happening here."

"I'm talking about testing my DNA for Dr. Simon's murder. You could've asked me for a hair sample. You didn't have to resort to deceit. I would've given it to you freely. But what hurts more is, after all we've been through together, that you could possibly believe I was a murderer." Quinn's chest rose and fell with hurried, frustrated breaths. "I want to know ... when you and I ... was it just to get a DNA sample from me? Is that why you let me take you in the hall like that? Were you just doing your job?"

"No, Quinn, I ... yes, I did take a sample, but not in the hallway, not when you think." A blush stained her cheeks as she thought of her back pressed up against the wall. "It was before, when you kissed me outside Kirill's office. That's when I took the sample."

Quinn looked at Tori, his heart beating a thunderous rhythm in his chest. When he'd heard Grant and Vitto laughing about it, he'd just assumed it'd been the last time they were together. To know she took the sample before she'd even known for sure that it was a Var who committed the act, hurt worse. Everything else that he'd been about ready to confess to her slipped away and he couldn't speak.

"Quinn, you tested fine. It's not you," she said, as if that made it all better. Her rounded eyes looked up at him.

Quinn frowned. "I know it wasn't me. I told you that, but obviously my word wasn't good enough for you, was it Tori?"

"No, science ... we have to logically deduce--" Tori tried to explain.

"This has nothing to do with science, Tori." Quinn didn't want to hear it. She was always about the work! Forgetting about him for work! Running out on him for work! Ignoring him for work! He was tired of being second to her job. "Not everything in the universe has to fit into a nice scientific package."

"But--"

"This has everything to do with us--you and me." Quinn's fingers lifted to her cheek, but did not caress. "It has to do with you not trusting me when I told you I didn't hurt Simon. You didn't believe that I just found him. After what we'd been through together--"

"What, I should trust you because we have sex? Because you..." Tori's face turned red with anger. She dropped her hands from her breasts to scream at him.

Quinn shot forward, grabbing her roughly in his arms. His hand slipped over her cheek, tangling back into her dark wet locks. He pressed her back into the rock, and growled viciously, "Is that all this is to you? Huh, Tori? Is this just sex? Am I just another conquest to fill your time on some planet? Fine, if that's what you want from me, that's exactly what you'll get."

Quinn wanted to scream with the pain rolling inside him. His lips pushed forward, taking her mouth in a bruising kiss that was meant to punish her for making him feel. He poured all his frustration onto her, prying her lips apart with his tongue, grinding so hard his teeth bumped into hers.

Tori's arms wound up to his shoulders. She pushed lightly to get him to back off. She tried to kiss him back, but he didn't allow it.

Mindless with rage, he freed himself from his clothes with one hand, still holding on to her head with the other. Letting his hard arousal free, he drew his lips back. Even now, he wanted her--needed her desperately. He felt a void when she wasn't around. It was getting worse as the days passed. He was under a spell, her spell, and he wanted to be free of it.

"Quinn," she whispered. When he looked at her, she didn't appear to be upset. She looked aroused. It was too much. Her words whimpered from her throat, begging him to continue. He couldn't stop if he wanted to. "Ah, Quinn, please. Now."

Lifting her up against the rock, he brought himself right next to her, supporting her with his hands. Her legs wrapped around his back. Her fingers clutched his shoulder, gripping tightly as she opened herself up for him. She pulled at his jaw, lifting his mouth up to hers so she could kiss him. Her kiss was tender compared to his. When he entered the warmth of her body, it was with an urgency they both felt.

"Quinn," she whispered, over and over. "Ah, Quinn, Quinn...."

Heat curled within them as they joined. He thrust, hard and sure within her, touching her deeply. Tori moaned into his mouth and he returned the sentiment twice as loud. His hips pumped wildly into hers, pressing her back. She couldn't escape, didn't want to try. The tension built, washing over her from between her thighs. His eyes possessed her as he stared deeply into her. When his body finally exploded inside her, she whimpered, holding onto him as she reached her own violent release.

A slow clap sounded over the bathing pool. "Wonderful show, my prince!"

Tori yelped in surprise, leaning to look over Quinn's shoulder. Her body had felt so wonderful pressed into his and now that pleasure drained as cool green eyes met hers from the shoreline. The man stood alone. He was shorter in stature for a Var male with long graying black hair that flowed freely over his shoulders. Even without the gray, she'd have been able to instantly tell his age. There was a strange carriage to him, as if he had power, respect, plans.

Quinn dropped her to her feet and quickly laced up his pants. For a moment, his bright blue eyes met hers. She saw the hard expression on his face, the tense working of his clenched jaw. She read a silent warning in his gaze and nodded. He turned his back on her to face the intruder.

Tori watched his muscles flex, as he took off his shirt and thrust it back at her. Grateful, she pulled it over her head. It was damp in spots and stuck to her thighs, but she didn't care, as she pulled the laces together to hide her nakedness. Pushing her wet hair back from her face, she tried to move to his side. Without even looking, his arm shot out and stopped her progress. He pushed her once more behind his back.

"Lord Myrddin," Quinn said, his voice flat. His head shifted as he nodded.

Lord Myrddin! Tori tried to lean over to get another look at the man. This time when Quinn pushed her back it wasn't as gentle. She gasped as she stumbled into the trickling water, wetting the shirt even more.

"My prince," Lord Myrddin answered.

Tori could hear the smirk in his words, the disrespect. Her body stiffened. Eyeing Quinn's naked back, she couldn't help feeling protected. She quietly leaned over to peek between his arm and side, angling her head so Quinn wouldn't hear her doing it. The man on shore hadn't moved.

"I'm curious, my prince. Aside from the most obvious," Lord Myrddin grinned at them with meaning, but the look was not pleasant, "what brings you to my shadowed marshes?"

Tori shivered. This man made her very nervous.

"We were on our way to see you," Quinn answered. His hand lifted to rest on his hip, unintentionally making it easier for her to see.

"Oh?" Lord Myrddin's eyes met hers and he nodded briefly. Quinn stiffened. "Why don't you let your lady out of hiding, my prince, and introduce us?"

"Quinn?" Tori whispered.

"My lady is not prepared for company. If my lord would be so kind as to come back later, I'd be happy to make the introduction at that time." Quinn's arm lowered and she frowned. His voice rang with authority, as he stepped forward. Tori followed behind him.

"Ah, if we are doing away with formality, then let's not pretend ignorance. I assume you are the Dr. Elliot, come to save us from ourselves?" Lord Myrddin asked, raising a brow.

"My brother, the king, requests you join him at the palace." Quinn didn't move and Tori thought it better than to speak.

"Three noble princes sent to request my presence?" The man laughed. "It sounds a little suspicious, don't you think? Why not send a missive to my home?"

"We tried that," Quinn said. "There was no response."

"Ah, so it wasn't a request, but an order," Lord Myrddin answered, waving his hand in the air. "How interesting. The new king thinks to order me, an elder. I've been in power longer than he's drawn breath."

"He is your king," Quinn stated in warning.

"Things have a way of changing, my prince," Lord Myrddin answered.

"Quinn?" Tori's voice shook as she touched his arm.

"Your father was a king. Now there was a man who knew how to rule. He was bold, courageous. He knew what had to be done and he did it, without second thoughts and without remorse. The Var people have waited for him to act, and yet Kirill has not." A large Var stepped onto the shore behind Myrddin.

"Quinn," Tori whispered again, edging closer. Again, he didn't answer, didn't turn to look at her.

"Instead," Lord Myrddin continued, ignoring her as well, "he takes a queen, weakening the Var throne and the Var future. Does he avenge his father by taking arms against the Draig? No, he makes friends with our ancient enemies, invites them into his home, makes them welcome, and talks peace in Attor's hall! He leads them onto my land, shows them our secrets."

"The king has his reasons for what he does." Quinn took another step toward shore and Tori stayed right behind him, touching his side lightly. "As for your land, this is the king's land by birthright and he can go where he pleases with whom he pleases. It was necessary, for the safety of our people as well as the Draig, to...."

"Take our weapon? Ruin our plans?" Lord Myrddin asked, smirking. "We can get another weapon and will. All you did was delay the inevitable. Mark my words, with or without your brother, the Draig race will be annihilated."

"To use that weapon would be to kill the Var as well as the Draig," Tori shot, moving forward. Quinn grunted in anger. His hand shot forward to stop her.

"Acceptable losses in the battle we face, my dear," Lord Myrddin answered. His cool green eyes shifted, darkening with rage and hate. Bitterly, he spat, "Tell me, my prince, are you life mate as well to this creature? It's hard to believe King Attor's line would've turned out so weak. It's a blessing he's not here to see it. Although, if he was here, Kirill would've never have married and the Draig would already be dead."

Another Var stepped out of the forest, and then another. Soon the shoreline was filled with them. In the back, Tori saw Vitto and Grant. They were bound and gagged. Their limp bodies didn't move and they were draped over the sides of a hideous looking creature. The beast had a center horn protruding from its skull, the eyes of a reptile, the face and hooves of a beast of burden, and the body comparable to that of a small elephant.

"Three princes all delivered up to me," Lord Myrddin laughed, prompting his men to do the same. "What a fortunate day this is ... for me."

Tori stared at her brother and Grant, feeling ill. She wanted to go to them, but her path was blocked by several burly Var soldiers. She glanced at Quinn. His darkened eyes met hers briefly. He was trying to tell her something, but she couldn't understand. She wasn't trained for these situations.

"Lord Myrddin," Tori said, trying to reason with him. "Please, let us go. You don't want this. We are scientists for the Human Intelligence Agency. If we disappear, they'll send an army after us to find out what happened. They already know about the cave and I've reported the black moss situation. Do you really want all those foreigners here, invading your planet, finding your secret laboratory within the cave? Please, I can help you. Tell us what happened in the lab, what you were trying to do, and we can try to fix it. If we don't this whole planet could be dead within a decade."

Everyone was quiet for a long time, staring at her. Tori swallowed, hoping they were considering her offer. Suddenly, Lord Myrddin burst out laughing. "My sweet lady, thank you for your offer to help. As it turns out, I planned on you helping me--along with those two there." He jerked his thumb at Vitto and Grant. "You're one of the reasons I'm here."

Tori paled.

"You're not going to disappear, Dr. Elliot, you're going to work for me." Lord Myrddin lifted his hand and motioned.

Quinn growled, partly shifted as he jumped up from the pool to the shore. His claws brandished like knives, he swung for Lord Myrddin's throat. Someone anticipated the move and shot Quinn in the side with a dart. He fell over, instantly weakened, barely drawing blood on Lord Myrddin's cheek. The elder didn't move from his place.

"You stupid..." Lord Myrddin cursed, touching his cheek. Seeing the blood, he kicked the fallen prince in the gut, hard.

Quinn grunted. Tori screamed. His eyes darted to her. She took a step back. Var men leapt into the pool, surrounding her. She tried to step away from them and only succeeded in walking straight back into one of them, getting herself caught.

"Let me go!" Tori demanded, kicking and struggling. "Quinn!"

Quinn grunted, but she couldn't see him. Tori fought harder. Lord Myrddin sighed and stepped over the shore to the strange mount. He gripped Vitto's head by the hair and lifted it up. Taking a blade from his belt, he whistled for attention. Tori saw the blade glint with sunlight and instantly went still with panic.

"Cooperate, Dr. Elliot," Lord Myrddin warned, not even needing to lay voice to the rest of the threat.

Tori shook violently, terrified beyond anything she'd ever felt. But, knowing Quinn was near brought her comfort. She turned to look for him. The shoreline was empty. He was gone.

Lord Myrddin dropped Vitto's head and stormed to the shore once more. He growled in outrage and, turning to the man closest to where Quinn had been, threw the knife into the man's heart. The Var soldier gasped and fell to his feet. No one moved to help him as he died almost instantly.

Pointing at the guards in the pool, he ordered, "Go! Find him. He's drugged so he couldn't have gotten too far."

The men who held her let go. She was too numb to move as they all ran off into the forest. The remaining guard stood on the shore, not moving to capture her.

Lord Myrddin's red face turned, as he pointed to the dead soldier and said, "Someone, get rid of him."

Tori shook, feeling faint. Her eyes watered as she stared at the shore. He'd left her. Quinn had left her.

"Come," Lord Myrddin said, his voice softening. "Don't let all this scare you, my lady. So long as you behave, you're to be a guest in my home. You'll be treated with kindness, given food, shelter."

"B-be-behave?" she stuttered, feeling very cold and wet. As he waved her forward again, she took a shaking step toward him. Better to use her legs than to be dragged.

"All in due time, Dr. Elliot," he soothed. "All in good time. Come, let us warm you first."

* * * *

Quinn pressed his body to the tree, gripping the trunk as he tried not to pass out. He was high off the ground, hidden in the branches. The drug they'd given him was potent, but at the moment his will was stronger. It took everything he had to keep from falling and thus getting himself caught.

Tori's pale, frightened face wouldn't leave him. She'd looked so fragile, so confused as she stared at him from the shallow pool. But, he thought with pride, she bravely tried to negotiate with Lord Myrddin and didn't let herself get captured without a fight. Quinn chuckled grimly and it was her memory alone that kept him holding on.

Chapter Eleven

Tori glared at Lord Myrddin, hating him with her entire being. He was an evil man. If she doubted it before, she knew so now. Slowly, she shook her head in firm denial. There was no way she could do what he asked of her. "Kill me if you will, but I can't do this for you. There is no way I'm going to have a hand in genocide."

"Yeah, you see, I'm not exactly sure what the word genocide means, Dr. Elliot," Lord Myrddin answered, waving his hand. His long purple cloak whirled around his feet as he walked. He was dressed similar to Quinn and his brothers, but his clothing was tight and had no laces that showed peeks of skin. Rings adorned his fingers and a silver clasp kept the long locks of his hair back from his face. From what she knew of him he had to be several hundred years old, perhaps one of the oldest Var she had yet to meet. By human estimation, he didn't look a day over forty. He was a handsome man--in a completely demented, went insane three hundred years ago, sort of way. He chuckled softly, and added, "And, honestly, I really don't care."

Tori's eyes narrowed in on him. They were in Lord Myrddin's castle home, in his dark study. Firelight glinted over them, giving the only light. The fireplace was huge, dominating the room with its presence. The dark stone reflected the mood of the man before her quite well. She'd seen similar castles before in earth history books. She felt small under the intimidating, high ceilings. No doubt that was the elder's intent when he designed it.

Lord Myrddin had several wives, many of whom had waited on her since her arrival. They walked around him on tiptoes, their eyes always on the floor as they simpered and bowed. They refused to speak to her, refused to help her. The pitiful creatures looked more like they were beaten into submission than respectful.

Tori shivered. He wanted to finish some experiment he'd started nearly a century ago. Only too willingly, did he tell her about how the original scientists had defied him, trapping their guard in the cage at the cave laboratory, next to the Draig man they'd been forced to use for experiments. Obviously, by the bones they'd discovered, the men hadn't been let out, but locked up and left to starve to death. The defiant scientists were captured and slowly tortured, before finally meeting their end.

Tori got the distinct impression that Lord Myrddin told her the story, in gruesome detail, to scare her. It worked. She was terrified. But how could she agree to murder a race of people? It went against everything she'd ever done as a scientist.

"Oh, all right," Lord Myrddin said, waving a nonchalant hand like he was giving in. Tori blinked, wondering what he was up to. "I tired to ask nicely, I even said please. However, if you insist on doing this the fun way, then I'll just have to play along."

"What do you mean?" Tori gulped. She felt the blood draining from her face. She could only imagine what this man would consider fun.

"Guards!"

Tori jolted as the door opened. She whirled around, panting in fear. Battered and bruised, Vitto, Grant, and Prince Reid were dragged into the room by several guards. Tori felt sick to her stomach. It was obvious they'd been through hell. Their hands were bound behind their backs and they looked as if they hadn't eaten for the three days they'd been at the castle. At least she'd been locked into a room with a bed and food. She waited for Falke, but he was missing. Terror struck her. Where was Prince Falke?

"Oh, tsk, tsk, why such the worried face, Dr. Elliot. Aren't you enjoying yourself? You wanted to play tough, so we're playing tough." Lord Myrddin walked past her, his hand gliding over her shoulder, making her jerk away from him. He merely chuckled, pleased, as he moved over to the men. He studied them for a moment, letting silence fall over the chamber, marred by heavy breathing and crackling fire. Finally, he glanced over his shoulder at her. "Isn't this what you wanted? What did you think would happen when you denied my simple request?"

"Killing is not a simple request," she whispered hoarsely.

"Oh, that's where you're wrong." Lord Myrddin's brow rose in challenge. He smiled and walked again across the room, not touching her this time as he passed near. Tori closed her eyes and shivered. She heard him behind her and moved to watch him draw a sword from the wall. He studied the sharp blade, letting the orange fire reflect off its shiny surface. "Killing is perhaps one of the simplest of acts, so easy to do, so impossible to reverse."

"You're a monster," Tori spat, glaring at him. She was too afraid to do much else, especially when he twisted the sword in his hand, leisurely showing that he knew how to use it.

"Yes, but that's beside the point, isn't it doctor?" Again he chuckled.

"Leave her alone, Myrddin," Reid growled, lurching forward against his restraints. "You have no quarrel with the humans."

The elder frowned and motioned to the guards. One guard grabbed Reid's head and the other kneed him in the stomach. The prince fell to the ground, moaning.

"So, Dr. Elliot," Lord Myrddin continued as if there had been no interruption. He lifted his sword and slowly pointed at each man in turn. "Which one of them will it be? Would you like to decide or shall I?"

Tori panted erratically, turning to look at the three prisoners. Her whole body shook. She couldn't take much more of this. The men's eyes met hers. Grant's were nearly swollen shut. Reid shook his head, telling her no, pleading with her not to give in. Vitto's lips parted, but she couldn't tell what he mouthed to her. She had no choice. She couldn't push Lord Myrddin any further, for she had not doubt he'd make good on his threats. Weak, her voice a breathless whisper, she said, "Put your blade back, my lord."

"Excuse me, doctor?" Lord Myrddin's voice boomed. "I couldn't hear."

"I said," she gritted, turning to glare at him though still shaking violently, "put back your blade."

"You'll do it?" he asked, swinging the sword back and forth lightly. Tori quickly nodded. A side of his lip curled up. "Very good, Dr. Elliot."

"I need Dr. Grant's and Dr. Vitto's help," Tori said, trying to sound calm as she lied. She could probably do it on her own, but she wouldn't let him know that. "Dr. Grant specializes in DNA research and Dr. Vitto is the only one who's been trained to run some of our equipment. We're a team and can work a lot faster if there are three of us. Otherwise, it could take me months, perhaps a year or more to do what you ask."

"Done," he said, motioning to the guards. They cut the two scientists free. Vitto and Grant landed on their hands and knees, moaning in unison. Tori rushed over to them, trying to examine their wounds without hurting them. Glancing up at Reid, she whispered, "And I want you to release Prince Reid and Prince Falke. They'll give you their word that nothing will happen to you for this."

"Ah, no." Lord Myrddin placed the sword back on the wall, laughing. "But, I do applaud your audacity in trying. I admire a woman with guts."

"Then I want you to let me tend their wounds and I want them fed. Either this, or you make your own damned weapon! Those are my terms." Tori stood, knowing there wasn't much she could do for Grant and her brother at the moment. She needed a medical laser, first aide kit, something.

"Very well, I'll humor you for now, Dr. Elliot. You may tend to them. But, if you don't make reasonable progress, I will be forced to renegotiate our deal." His voice lowered, as he stepped forward. His face drew close to hers and he looked at her lips, eyeing them as if he would kiss her. Softly, his mouth a hairsbreadth away from hers, he said, "I don't relish hurting you, Dr. Elliot, for you're a very lovely woman and I abhor scarring beautiful things." His mouth moved to her ear. "But you don't need your legs to be able to do your work. Are we understood?"

Tori nodded, unable to look at him directly when he stood so close.

"Good." Lord Myrddin turned to the guards and ordered, "Take her and the two scientists to the lab so that they may get started. Show Prince Reid to his ... room."

"But you said..." Tori began in protest as Reid was roughly dragged off. He looked so battered, so defeated.

"I said you could tend them, Dr. Elliot. I didn't say when. You'll have your chance, just as soon as you give me what I want. It lies on your head now. If they die, it will be your fault. So I suggest you work fast." Lord Myrddin turned his back on them and walked to his desk. The guards gripped her arm and jerked her forward when she didn't move fast enough.

"Men like you always get what's coming to them!" she screamed, glaring hotly at him. She wished with all her heart Quinn was with her. She wasn't sure what he'd be able to do, but his nearness would bring her comfort. No, that was selfish. If he was here, he'd be as battered as the others. It was a good thing he ran when he did.

Lord Myrddin laughed. His dark words followed her as she was forced down a narrow hall. "Sorry my dear, but in reality they really don't."

* * * *

Tori looked over her shoulder at the Var guard. He was standing on the other side of the bars to their giant cell, watching her through the iron strips. He stared at her, had been staring at her since they came to the "laboratory." She knew well the hunger in his eyes. He wanted her and that terrified her. Slowly, he licked his lips, causing her to shiver in fear and repulsion. She thought of Quinn. When she closed her eyes, she could almost feel him near her. Her heart called out to him, wanted him. Her brain feared for him and silently begged that he stay away--far from harm.

"Ignore him, Tori," Vitto said, placing a hand on her shoulder. She turned her wide eyes to him and nodded, before moving to where Grant sat. They were still pretty banged up, but after being fed and cleaned up, they looked better--if not a little weak.

The laboratory was in the dungeon of Lord Myrddin's castle. She had no doubt that he'd placed them there on purpose. The stone was dusty and smelled bad, hardly an ideal scientific environment, but they could make due.

They'd walked past Reid in his cell to get to theirs. The man's eyes pleaded with them not to do it. But, how could she not? She couldn't condemn them to death. But, if she did, she'd be condemning a whole race to death. Could she live with herself if she let Vitto, Grant and the two princes die? Could she live with herself if she let a whole race of innocent people die? All she could do was pray for a miracle, pray that Quinn had gotten away. Thinking of it, she wanted to cry. Her eyes watered and there was an ache deep in her chest. Quinn might already be dead.

"We can't do this," Tori said, leaning over Grant and pretending to watch what he was doing. He was looking up the sequencing for the black moss, trying to figure out what the scientists before them had done. The equipment they were given was old, more than likely taken from the laboratory within the caves.

The guard made an aggressive sound. She turned to him, realizing he'd heard her, and said quickly, "This equipment is old. It's going to take longer. Ask Lord Myrddin if he has anything newer that we may use."

The guard stared at her for a long time.

"Fine, but when he asked why we can't work faster, I'm telling him you didn't report our request." Tori shrugged and turned her face away toward Grant. She closed her eyes, stiff, waiting.

"Very well," the guard said at length. She sighed, glancing back over her shoulder to see him leaving.

Tori grabbed a piece of paper, and wrote, 'Room bugged? Don't talk. Grant, need to get black moss sequencing and work to see if we can kill it. Vitto and I need to make show of trying to make progress.'

Both men nodded.

Tori took a deep breath and began tearing the paper into tiny pieces, dropping them around the dirty floor. Aloud, she said, "The guard will be back soon. I need to know what you guys think."

"You're the boss," Grant said. "We'll do what you tell us."

"Vitto?" Tori asked.

"Yeah, Tor, whatever you say," Vitto answered.

"All right you guys, I have no wish to die in here. Let's just do this and hope that we can get off this planet before the damned weapon is released. Afterwards, no one will ever know what we did."

"You're right, Tori, we don't belong here. This isn't our problem," Vitto answered. "HIA made us come."

"Yeah," Grant said. "It's not our problem. They dug their own graves. I just want to go home now."

"Do you think Lord Myrddin will let us out of here?" Vitto asked, sounding scared, though his face was hard as he looked at his sister. They all knew the little play they put on was just that--a play.

"If not ... if we have to stay here, better to be at the devil's side than in front of him." Tori took a deep breath. She wanted Quinn. She wanted him now! "If we do as he says, he'll likely keep us alive. So, let's make him happy and get to work."

The three nodded silently. Tori and Vitto moved to begin the tests to see where the scientists left off. Grant turned back to the computer, trying to pull up old files. They didn't speak again.

* * * *

Quinn was tense with anger, as he hid out of view of Lord Myrddin's castle fortress. The black stone rose over the marshes, forbiddingly covered in a green moss, looking as if the old stone grew up from the swamplands surrounding it. His helplessness in the situation ate at him, until he couldn't sleep, couldn't eat, and could think of nothing but her--Tori.

He remembered her face, as she stood in the stream. Her eyes had begged him for protection, but he lay helpless on the ground. He'd been unable to save her and he cursed himself because of it. If he hadn't of been so preoccupied with trying to figure out her feelings for him, he could've focused on what happened around him. He'd like to think that, had his head been clear, he'd have been able to protect her. But, he'd failed.

Remorseful, he remembered his words to her about the earth custom of killing and bringing forth a ferocious teddy bear as a date offering. He'd told her it was good to choose a man who could defend her against such dreaded beasts. It was good advice when he gave it, and it was good advice still. He obviously wasn't the best person to protect her.

When he was next to her, emotion took over and he didn't think straight.

He could only assume that is what King Attor meant when he spoke of love being a weakness. The way he felt, the way he could hardly concentrate, the way she constantly danced in his brain--it wasn't good. It was turning him into a madman. He couldn't afford to be so preoccupied with her. She didn't belong in his world. She didn't belong with him. He hadn't wanted to admit it before, but now he had no choice. When her assignment was over, Dr. Tori Elliot needed to go. It was better for both of them if she did, for she'd be safe and he'd regain his sanity.

Quinn frowned. He hated that he'd been forced to leave her, but he wouldn't have done any of them any good by getting himself caught. The drug Lord Myrddin shot him with took well over a day to wear off. He hid up in the tree as long as he could, before deciding it was safe to come down. Shifting into his cougar form, he'd found a small hiding spot within the forest to lie down. He'd slept, unable to help himself, as the drug finally took over his system.

When he awoke, disorientated and with a massive headache, he'd stumbled his way back to the Var palace, remaining on all fours. Even with the added strength and speed of his cougar form, the walk took him three times longer than it should have. Kirill met him at the side gate and it was less than an hour before they were ready to leave again.

Peering across the forest from where he crouched, Quinn slowly nodded at his brother. Kirill was shifted to a black panther. His expression was rigid with anger. He knew the king feared for the captured princes and the human scientists. None one of them suspected Lord Myrddin would go as far as he did.

Quinn's head still hurt, but sheer determination kept him from paying attention to it. A roar built in his throat, but he held it back. He was so angry his limbs shook. His brothers were inside Lord Myrddin's castle. Tori was in there. His heart squeezed painfully in his chest. He felt sick, hearing her voice echo in his head.

Quinn....

Glancing to his other side, he nodded at Treven who was in human form. The soldier nodded back. Treven was a tiger shifter and one of the best soldiers they had. Only the three of them had come. If Lord Myrddin watched the palace, it wouldn't do to have an army of vicious cats marching out of it.

Slowly, all three shifters crept forward, ready to pounce. Jumping up, Kirill and Quinn each landed on a guard, taking their sharp teeth to their throats to keep them from crying out. They didn't break the skin, but held them pinned to the ground in warning. Treven instantly injected the men with a sleeping agent. The brothers held them, teeth on necks, until they drifted off. There was no reason to kill unless their hand was forced. When this was over, each of Lord Myrddin's men would have a fair hearing as to what their part was in this treachery.

The princes pulled back and shifted back to man, naked and proud as they moved forward through the castle gates. They were used to losing their clothes each time they shifted in battle. Only their eyes remained as they were, the pupils bent with the superior vision of the cat.

* * * *

Quinn walked on all four paws down the long corridor to the dungeon. The princes spent a lot of time visiting Lord Myrddin's home with their father when they were children and he found his way around with ease. Sniffing the air, he stalked low to the ground, moving forward with deadly grace as he passed an empty cell. He knew his brother was close--could smell that he was.

Reaching a paw forward, he swiped, reaching around the corner to grab a guard's leg. The man yelped softly in surprise and didn't fall. Quinn shifted, letting go as he stood. When he turned the corner completely, Reid stood with his arm poking out from between the bars, his elbow locked over the man's throat. In his free hand he held a sword from the man's waist.

"Took you long enough," Reid grumbled. A large purpling bruise covered the side of his face, swelling one eye shut. His lip was swollen and crusted with blood, but they managed to twitch into a welcoming smile. He tightened his hold on the guard's throat until the man passed out.

"Sacred Cats, Reid!" Quinn answered in kind, grabbing the blade from his brother and taking it to the lock. "You smell worse than a rotting ceffyl floating in the shadowed marshes."

"He looks about your size. Want his clothes?" Reid asked.

Quinn took the unconscious guard from him and dragged him into the cell. "Where's Tori?"

"Myrddin's forcing her to do some kind of experiment for him. Come on," Reid ran down the long hall. Quinn didn't bother to get dressed as he followed naked behind him. Suddenly, Reid stopped and motioned.

Quinn sniffed, moving forward. Claws drew from his fingers. His heart fell from his chest. Fear like he'd never known it gripped him in its clutches. He smelled blood-- Tori's blood.

Chapter Twelve

"No!" Tori screamed, shaking her head as she tried to throw her body between Grant and the Var guard. Her eyes flew to Lord Myrddin. "Stop, we'll do it! We said we'll do it! I wasn't complaining. But we need better equipment."

Lord Myrddin's brow rose on his rigid face. Tori pointed at the guard. A low growl sounded in the back of the man's throat.

"I don't know what he said, but all I asked for was better equipment," Tori said, keeping between Grant and the Var.

"But you can do it?" Lord Myrddin asked.

Tori nodded. "Yes. I have to run some tests, but I can do it."

She wasn't lying. The scientists who worked before them had completed their assignment, only they forgot to tell Lord Myrddin about it. They had engineered the perfect biological killer, genetically altering the swampland's natural vegetation to produce the black moss. They'd nicknamed it the Black Crawl, because it crept up slowly, spreading underground through the planet's crust and mantle, sapping the soil of nutrients like a parasite. Already the entire planet could be infected with it. Soon crops would die, water would become undrinkable, and then the whole planet would be a dead zone. The scientists must have known that it would take at least a hundred years for the black moss to grow to such an amount to be detected aboveground. It could've been why they ran away. No doubt Lord Myrddin wouldn't have been happy with their time frame.

"Back off," Myrddin ordered the guard. The man instantly stepped back. The elder stepped forward, his claw retracted from his index finger as he walked. His long purple cloak drifted behind him, fluttering. "How long?"

"A month," Tori lied.

Lord Myrddin sneered. He took his claw, slashing her face. Tori gasped, feeling the pain of the cut. She cupped her cheek in her hand, stumbling back. Again, he asked, "How long?"

Tori wasn't so quick to answer. She swallowed. "I don't...."

"Three days," Grant stated from behind her back. Lord Myrddin turned to the man. Tori shut her eyes tight. "A month with this equipment here, but we can most likely have it done in about three days if we get to that cave laboratory."

Tori knew Grant was right. Only at the cave could they stop the source of the moss and thus the contamination of the entire Var and Draig populations. Lord Myrddin was mad to think he could play God, choosing to kill one race and spare another. Biological weapons didn't discriminate like people did.

"Gather whatever you need," Lord Myrddin stated.

"Now?" Tori asked, blood seeping between her fingers from the cut.

"Is that a problem, Dr. Elliot?" Lord Myrddin asked.

"No, no problem." Tori motioned to Grant and Vitto. They began gathering supplies.

Suddenly, a loud roar sounded from the passageway. Tori blinked, turning to see Quinn running naked toward the cell. For a moment, she was stunned, unable to move from her spot on the floor as she watched him. His glorious body leapt into the air, shifting with tan fur as he aimed for Myrddin.

"Tell me why I shouldn't rip your treacherous heart from your chest!" Quinn growled, remaining at a half shift. The elder turned, striking Quinn in the side to fight off the attack.

"Quinn!" Tori yelled, looking around for a way to help him. It all happened so fast, she could hardly keep up. Lord Myrddin's and Quinn's bodies moved with liquid grace as they fought. Quinn shot forward, swiping at Myrddin's neck and drawing a small bead of blood. Myrddin growled. His age and strength was pitted against the younger fighter's passion. Quinn gained the upper hand, but barely. Myrddin's claws hit his arm, drawing blood. The prince didn't seem to notice.

Tori screamed, ready to jump on Myrddin's back and defend Quinn. She braced herself, ready for an opening. A guard went flying by the passageway behind the bars. Reid burst around the corner to help his brother against Myrddin.

Their lecherous Var guard, forgotten in that brief moment of insanity, grabbed her from behind, holding an extended claw to her artery. The guard roared to get their attention as he angled Tori's body for everyone to see. His voice a deadly growl, he said, "Let him go, or this one loses her life."

Tori shivered, panting, "Ah, Quinn."

"Step back," the guard spat. His claw tapped against her flesh and she was too scared to move. A weak sound left her throat. Her round eyes found Quinn's steady gaze. She drew strength from him.

Quinn's face was hard and she knew he was worried. With a loud growl, he let go of Myrddin. Tori whimpered again as the guard jostled her before him.

Tori's heart soared to know he'd come for her. But, she couldn't go with him. Not now. She needed access to the cave laboratory, to the information stored there. The easiest way was for Lord Myrddin to take her there and give her access. If she left, he could possibly seal the cave off and dump the evidence. Then all hope for Qurilixen would be lost.

The guard dragged her backwards, until they were close to Lord Myrddin.

"Come," Lord Myrddin said to Vitto and Grant.

"No," Tori whispered. The Var growled in warning. "I don't need them anymore. I can do the rest myself."

The guard yanked Tori out of the cell. She watched as Lord Myrddin locked all four men inside. Their hard eyes followed them. Her lips trembled, as she mouthed the word, "Quinn."

"Don't worry," Lord Myrddin said to his new prisoners. His laughter was a cruel and heartless sound. She watched Quinn disappear from sight as she was pulled down the hall. "I'll send my welcoming committee down to deal with you all in a moment."

Tori gasped, struggling to be free. The guard struck her in the back of the head, knocking her completely unconscious.

* * * *

Quinn gripped the bars of the cell, shaking them violently. He watched in helplessness as Tori was again taken from him. Suddenly, her whimpers stopped. He froze, terrified. He shook the bars with a renewed force, roaring in outrage. His only hope was that Kirill would find and stop Lord Myrddin in time.

His heart thumped painfully in his chest. Her cheek had been marred with blood and she was pale, too pale. But, Sacred Cats, if she hadn't looked good! Just seeing her alive gave him comfort.

"Here."

Quinn turned to Vitto who held out a lab coat. He looked down, realized he was still naked, and slipped the coat over his shoulders. "We need to get out of here."

"We've looked. That's the only way," Grant answered, pointing at the locked door.

"We can't just stay here ... Tori," Quinn began.

"Is Kirill with you?" Reid asked.

"Treven and Kirill are with Falke. He was being tortured. I told them to get him home. They're gone." Quinn swallowed. Again, he hit the bars, shaking them violently. "I have to get to Tori!"

"We can't," Grant inserted. "Not yet."

Quinn turned on him in outrage. "What do you mean, we can't!"

Grant looked helplessly at Reid. Quinn was ready to pounce. Reid came forward and placed a hand on his brother's arm.

"What do you mean?" Reid asked, calmer.

"Tori wouldn't want us to. She knows what she's doing," Vitto said, hesitating as Quinn's passionate eyes turned on him. "She still feels bad about Simon and she thought to protect us. Besides, Lord Myrddin's taking her to the caves, to the laboratory there."

"The black moss is another biological weapon created by Myrddin's scientists about a hundred years ago," Grant interjected. Quinn exchanged a look with his brother. "It has spread beneath your planet's surface, pretty much dormant, but its growth rate is starting to accelerate. First, it will contaminate your water and soil, eating away at it like a parasite, then your vegetation and then, finally, when it has no where else to go, it'll begin to eat animals ... us, anything organic that isn't already dead. By that time, it will be everywhere. Anything that touches it will die. This planet will look like the shadowed marshes, but worse. Tori knows if she doesn't stop it, this whole planet is dead. This stuff can lay dormant for hundreds of years. Nothing will ever thrive here again."

"How long have you known for sure?" Quinn asked, hard. His heart beat in fear--fear for Tori, fear for his people. How could he choose between the two? His heart instantly said her, but he'd seen the way she mourned for Dr. Simon. If he saved her, only to watch everything else he loved die, she would die as well. She would never live with the guilt, and she'd possibly never forgive him. That quality, that selflessness, was one of the reasons he loved her.

Quinn froze. He felt the color drain from his face. Love? Did he...? He took a deep breath, then another. Yes. He loved her. He did. He loved her. The truth smacked him in the chest for a fool. He should've known it all along, ever since the hall when she walked in on him and Linzi. He hadn't been able to think of another woman since. It explained why he was crazy with thoughts of her, why she invaded every one of his dreams. He loved her. And he wasn't able to save her.

"After the initial tests we ran on the black moss came back, we suspected it was a threat, but we weren't sure how bad or where it came from. We thought it might be an ecological mutation which usually are harmless if not a little annoying. Ecological mutations are usually the cause of a natural imbalance that's easily corrected. But, then, when we saw the cave, we knew it was man-made." Vitto crossed over to the table and lifted the up a stack of data. "Here's all the information you need."

"But," Quinn said, feeling helpless. He loved her. He loved Dr. Tori Elliot. He was going to lose her. His brain ran rampant as he tried to concentrate. He tried to focus, tried to push her from his heart, but she wouldn't go. This is what his father had meant. This was the insanity King Attor had always warned his sons about. Reaching forward, he took the data from Vitto, unable to read it as it blurred before his eyes. "We can't risk her life, not for this. There has to be another way."

"Not in the time frame we have," Vitto answered. The man looked pained by the admission. Quinn noticed his pale face and his shaking hands. This man cared for Tori, deeply. He'd been too jealous to realize the depth of it before.

Reid stepped forward and gave him a questioning look. Quinn shook his head and refused to answer it. Now was not the time for one of Reid's lectures. Lifting his chin and steeling himself, Quinn demanded, "Tell us everything."

* * * *

Tori stared at the underground lab, absently feeling the dried blood on her cheek. The wound was superficial, but it still ached. The moss looked thicker, blacker, than the last time she'd seen it. A strange smell was in the air. She was almost afraid to walk inside.

"I'm curious, doctor, what is it they were working on for me?" Lord Myrddin asked, coming up behind her. He studied his hand, watching his claw grow and retract before his eyes. "Darts? A pill?"

Tori took a deep breath, and whispered honestly, "Death."

Lord Myrddin laughed.

"Death of your whole planet." Tori turned to him. The guard was outside, watching the entrance to the cave, so they were alone. "Unless I stop it, this whole planet will die and all that will be left for you to rule will be a wasteland of your own making."

"You fail to see the grand design, Dr. Elliot. Those who swear allegiance to me will live. That's why I need an antidote as well as the disease." His eyes turned to her, piercing into her, making her feel ill.

"Diseases such as these can never be contained. They mutate, lay dormant for years. Soon the cure we have won't be the right one." Tori's gaze pleaded with him. She moved as if to touch him, but pulled back. "Please, reconsider."

"Unless you help me, all your friends will die. Think of the hero's welcome you'll receive as you work for me, curing the poor Var peasants of their sickness. You'll be famous, revered as a savior. You'll have more power and respect than you could ever dream possible." Lord Myrddin walked past her and a predatory growl sounded in the back of his throat. She blinked, watching as a computer screen flipped over in the wall. It stood white and clean against the mossy background. The Var growled again, speaking in his native language. The computer turned on. Then, gesturing for her to proceed, he moved back.

Tori's steps were hesitant as she crossed over the floor. Her body shook. All around her the moss felt alive, like it twitched, straining for them. Lord Myrddin's hand lifted to touch her cheek. He stroked her gently, running his fingers over her hair. His lips brushed over the cut, kissing it lightly. "Do this, Dr. Elliot, and you will have my protection. I will be king and you will live like a queen."

"I can't concentrate with you talking," she said darkly, staring at the screen so hard she couldn't see it. Lord Myrddin chuckled and turned his back on her, obviously confident that she wasn't a threat.

Tori glanced around for a weapon. Seeing a long bar on the ground, she grabbed it. Without a moment's hesitation, she swung for Myrddin's head. Mid-swing, he turned, but was too late. The bar hit him in the temple. He stumbled to the side but righted himself. Tori swung again and again, thinking of Quinn trapped in the prison, as she hit him in the shoulder, the ribs, the wrist. She heard a bone crack and stopped.

Lord Myrddin fell to his knees, dripping with blood. Tori gasped for breath, adrenaline pumping through her veins. Myrddin's eyes were glazed when he looked up at her. Hesitating slightly, she swung again, hitting his head. She heard a crack, before watching him fall to the floor.

"Oh, God," she gasped, getting nauseous. She panted, shaking violently at what she had done. The metal bar slipped from her fingers. She'd never hurt another living thing in her life. She didn't think she had it in her. "Oh, oh, God, I'm sorry. I'm sorry. I'm so sorry."

Swallowing, she hurried before the computer and skimmed through the data until she found was she was looking for. The scientists had known what they'd done and had left her the clues to the cure. She glanced over her shoulder, making sure Lord Myrddin was still down.

"A ring? They left a ring?" she mumbled, confused. Then, she remembered having taken a large metal circle off one of the desks. It would be at the palace.

Lord Myrddin moaned behind her. She spun on her heels to look down at him. His hand shot out to grab her ankle. He moaned again. To her horror, the black moss spread over his face and body, drawn to the wounds on him. She kicked and his weakened grip loosened. He screamed, as the moss ate him alive.

Tori ran from the lab, blindingly trying to see across the darkened cave. Hearing footsteps approaching, she hid behind a rock. The guard passed her, his body outlined by the light coming from the lab as he moved inside. Tori made a run for it, bumping and tripping her way until she saw the lighted entrance. Her limbs shook as she pulled herself up through the hole.

"Stop!" the guard shouted behind her. Tori ran harder, trying to make the entrance to the cave. She stumbled through the large cavern to the narrow opening that would lead outside. "You *gwobr,* get back here!"

Tori paused at the entrance. It was a long way down. Before she could turn back around a hand pushed at her from behind, knocking her out of the cave. She fell through the air, screaming as she plummeted to her death.

* * * *

Quinn heard the sound of Tori's cry through the forest. He ran faster, his body sleek as it stretched out on all four paws. Thankfully, his brother had not listened to him and sent Treven back with Falke. He could've kissed Kirill as he unlocked the cell door. Instead, he'd run past, instantly following the trail of Lord Myrddin and Tori.

Quinn knew it was wrong, but he chose Tori. He chose her life over everything else he held dear. Together they would find a way to fight whatever madness Myrddin had started. But, he chose to save her. How could he do anything less? He'd just have to pray to all their gods that after she was safe, she could reverse whatever Lord Myrddin had done.

His heart pounded. The screaming didn't stop. Coming to the cave entrance, he saw Tori falling, her arm flailing in the air. His heart stopped beating. He surged forth, shifting in mid jump as he reached for her. Her body jolted, knocking hard into him, cracking his rib as they collided. Tori landed on his stomach as they hit the ground.

Quinn touched her face and then looked up at the cave. He saw Lord Myrddin's man looking down at them.

"Myrddin?" he growled, assessing that she was all right.

"Dead," she whispered, her lips trembling, her eyes glazed.

"Don't move," Quinn ordered. "The others are behind me."

Tori nodded, shaken, scared, and confused. Quinn shifted, climbing easily up the rocky incline. The guard dropped a rock, barely missing him. She watched Quinn's body go over the side, into the cave. Shouts sounded overhead, but she could barely make them out through her numbed brain.

Tori trembled, unable to move. Her legs were like jelly. Quinn had saved her. But it wasn't just nearly dying that frightened her. When she looked at her hands, she saw blood--Myrddin's blood. It was dotted over her. Tears filled her eyes.

"Dr. Elliot?"

She blinked, looking up. Reid stared at her from swollen eyes filled with concern. Kirill was behind him. Her hands shaking, she pointed up, barely able to make the gesture from her place on the ground. Kirill and Reid shifted, dropping their clothes as they climbed up to join their brother.

The guard's body was thrown out of the cave before the cats reached the top. Tori heard him thud behind her. She felt dizzy, faint. Blackness swam in her head and she welcomed it, falling over onto her side.

Chapter Thirteen

Quinn watched Tori as she slept. His body lounged next to her on the bed. They were in her suite and he refused to leave her side once the castle physicians were finished examining her. He would've stayed for the examination, but they kicked him out for hovering as they worked.

He ran a light hand over the bandage on her cheek. The cut was clean and would heal. It had been sealed with a medical laser. Aside from a few bruises and the trauma of what she'd been through, she was fine. Tori hadn't stirred since he carried her home. It had been quite a sight, the naked prince carrying the fallen doctor through the front gates of the palace. He chuckled lightly, remembering the stunned faces and hurried whispers.

Falke was in bed. He'd been cut up pretty badly, but would mend with time. Reid was up and around, though the last Quinn had seen him he was being attended by two harem girls, whining like a baby for attention. He smiled at that. Reid would never change. Dr. Vitto and Dr. Grant were given medical attention as well. They were a little sore, but would mend.

As he stared at Tori, Quinn knew what he felt for her was real. He'd been willing to risk his people to save her. They might still be at risk. Closing his eyes, he whispered, "Please, Tori. Wake up, baby, wake up."

A soft knock sounded on the door. Quinn sat up on the bed and looked across the suite. Vitto came in, his arm in a sling. The prince nodded at him in silent greeting.

"How is she?" Vitto asked, his voice soft with concern. "Has she moved?"

Quinn shook his head in denial. He watched the worry and stress pass over the man's face. It was clear he cared for her. Moving to stand, he said, "I'll leave you two alone."

Vitto nodded. He went to the bed, sitting by Tori's side. His hand reached out to stroke the bandage over her cheek.

Walking out of the room was hard, but Quinn forced himself to go. As he shut the door, he heard Vitto whisper, "I love you, Tor, but so help me if you ever pull a stunt like that again, I'm going to make you rue the day you were born."

* * * *

Tori yawned, blinking as thick velvet drapes came into focus. Rubbing her eyes, she sat up. A moment's confusion passed through her, until she remembered the caves. She glanced down at her hands, surprised to find them clean.

Shaking, she looked around and threw the covers off her legs. She was alone and she was naked. Weakly, she crawled to the end of the bed, moving to grab a pile of clothes that had been left for her. The cross laced shirt of blue with gold embroidery fit snug to her skin, but she didn't care.

She slipped into the pants as she stood from the edge of the bed, lacing them as she stumbled barefoot across the suite. Her mind focused, grasping at the work she must do so she didn't have to stop and think of other things.

"Siren," she called, her voice hoarse. "I need you to page Dr. Vitto and Dr. Grant. Tell them I require their immediate assistance."

"Yes, Dr. Elliot," the sultry mainframe answered. "Locating Dr. Vitto and Dr. Grant. Page complete."

"Thanks," Tori answered in growing distraction. "And, Siren, one more thing?"

"Yes, Dr. Elliot?"

"Prince Quinn, is he ... hurt?"

"I'm sorry, Dr. Elliot, that information is restricted to Level one security clearance."

"Damn it, Siren! Just tell me," Tori yelled. "Are his life functions normal?"

There was no answer.

"Fine, I'll go find out for myself." Tori stormed across the suite and moved to pull open the door. It wouldn't budge. She flicked the lock, locking and then unlocking it. She pulled the handle. It still didn't move.

"I'm sorry, Dr. Elliot," Siren purred. "But, you're not very polite. I believe you owe me an apology. And, just between us girls, why don't you tell me what's bothering you. I'm programmed with advanced psychiatric functions."

Tori would've laughed if she wasn't trapped in a room, held hostage by a sensitive computer who wanted to psychoanalyze her. Could this assignment get any more bizarre? Suddenly, she did laugh. "Okay, Siren, fine. You want to talk, let's talk. But first, I want DNA access."

"Granted, Dr. Elliot," Siren answered.

Tori smiled in grim satisfaction. She walked over to her bags and pulled out a sheet of paper. It was Quinn's DNA sequencing. She'd taken it from Grant's room and kept it. She knew it was a little strange, but to a scientist it was almost as good as a picture of him.

"Siren, please tell me where I can find the matching carrier to this DNA." Tori held the paper up.

"Match sequence found in harem, Dr. Elliot," Siren purred. "Identifying subject as ... I'm sorry Dr. Elliot. That information is restricted to level one security."

"That's perfectly all right," Tori answered. She felt like her heart was ripped out of her chest. Quinn was in the harem? Her head felt faint, dizzy. The suite spun around.

"Dr. Elliot, would you like to have that talk now?" Siren inquired.

Tori nodded, turned around, and fell into a crumpled heap on the floor.

* * * *

Quinn pushed the harem girl off his arm as he studied Reid. His bother, lying naked on this stomach, was enjoying the administering hands of three very pretty, very naked women. Quinn glanced over the women. They didn't do anything for him. All he could think about was Tori.

"Mm, Quinn, you should really try this," Reid groaned. His lips curled into a sheepish grin. "Mm, a little lower ... ah, that's it. Right there."

Two women massaged Reid's backside. Quinn turned away. It wasn't a particular memory he wanted to keep.

"Dr. Elliot wake up?" Reid asked, before groaning. "Ah, easy, ea-sy. I'm delicate merchandise, you know."

"Sorry, my lord," a harem girl pouted. "Is this better?"

"Ah! Why you naughty little..." Reid stopped talking amidst the women's giggling.

"You're busy. I'll go." Quinn stepped away from him, not daring to turn back around and see. Truth be told, he'd only come to the harem to see Reid because he had no other place to go. Falke was unconscious. Kirill was sleeping with his wife. Dr. Vitto was with Tori and Dr. Grant was being attended by Linzi. Thinking of Vitto's words, he paused. He'd heard it for himself. Vitto loved Tori.

"My lord, are you injured as well?"

Quinn blinked. It took a moment for him to realize two women were at his side. One boldly grabbed his shaft, as the other pressed her body firmly along his back. Reid chuckled knowingly behind him.

Quinn let them touch him for a moment, wondering if he should try to sleep with them. However, as they continued to fondle him, his body didn't stir. He felt nothing for them--not even the slightest hint of arousal. He frowned, swinging around to his brother.

"Sacred Cats!" Quinn growled, his eyes flashing with fire.

Reid jerked up in surprise. "Quinn? What is it? What's wrong?"

Quinn roared and stomped out of the harem, not bothering to answer.

* * * *

Tori tried to concentrate. Her backside was sore and she swore Siren must have jolted her with a laser beam when she passed out. When she pulled herself off the floor, Siren was claiming innocence, but her door was unlocked. Her heart broke, thinking of Quinn in the harem, but she had more important matters to take care of first.

Turning to Vitto, she smiled weakly and handed him the metal ring. "From what I remember, if we melt this and inject it into the ground near the caves it should work in killing off the moss. It should at least buy us enough time to analyze the properties and make sure it's all gone. The moss is supposed to be completely connected. I'm guessing the moss under the rock is where it's been seeping up from the ground."

"Tori," Vitto began. "We--"

Tori shook her head. "No, I don't want to discuss it. I just want to get this taken care of. I'm just ready for this assignment to be over."

* * * *

"Tori? Can I come in?"

Tori turned around in her chair, pushing back from the table. She wore a robe. It was held shut by a belt, but fell open to reveal her legs. Her heart skipped to hear Quinn's voice and she didn't bother to cover herself. Pushing her wet hair back from her face, she looked up at him. He stood in the door to her suite.

"I knocked, you didn't answer," he said, stepping in. He hesitated by the door, staring at her, letting his eyes roam down over her body.

Tori wanted to memorize every detail of him. She never wanted to forget a single moment of their time together.

They'd finished the antidote and were leaving in the morning to try it out. The preliminary tests in the lab were remarkable. Within an hour, the contaminated soil samples were restored to prime topsoil. If everything worked out, the three scientists could be going home by the end of the week.

The HIA work was finished, all except the final report. Tori could write that from her notes on the ship that would come to pick them up. Qurilixen, hopefully, would survive the black moss. And, if the moss ever came back, King Kirill could hire a new team to monitor the situation. She would be leaving him complete documentation for just such a case.

"Kirill wanted me to tell you that he's keeping everyone away from the caves until they've been treated." Quinn took a step forward and again hesitated. He turned, shutting the door softly behind him. "He'd also like to extend his gratitude to you and your colleagues for all that you've done for us."

Tori pushed to her feet, taking a step toward him and then another. Her robe closed around her legs. "What about you? What are you thinking?"

"I wish to thank you as well," he whispered. He looked like he wanted to say more, but didn't.

Tori nodded. She was suddenly drawn forward into his arms, as she rushed over the distance to be near him. Tears entered her eyes as threw her arms around his neck. She wasn't sure why she was crying, she just was.

"I killed him," she whispered, forlorn and so very lost. A dam broke within her and only in Quinn's arms did she feel safe. "I killed him. I only meant to stop him and I killed him instead."

"He deserved it. I would have done the same," Quinn whispered, stroking the wet hair down her back. Her shoulders trembled violently.

"It's not my decision to make," Tori sniffed. "I can't play God. I can't! I-I killed him."

"Shhh," Quinn hushed. "You did what you had to do. You saved a lot of people."

"No, you don't understand, Quinn," she tried to pull away but he didn't let her. His arms held her tighter and she let him, needing his comfort more than anything. "I'm a scientist. I'm supposed to save lives, make them better. I-I need you to kiss me. Just kiss me, Quinn, please."

The fight drained out of her limbs. She pressed her mouth to his, searing him with her passionate kiss. Everything she'd been through since coming to Qurilixen rushed over her, overwhelming her. The only thing good she could find in the whole mess of emotions was Quinn.

"Ah," she gasped, pulling her mouth away, panting for breath. Her hands skimmed over his body, tearing at his shirt as she pushed him across the suite to the bed. "I need you to make me feel. I need to feel anything but sadness. I just want to forget."

Quinn didn't resist. His hand dove into her hair, bringing her lips once more to his. She moaned as his long tongue rolled into her mouth, making her knees weak. Her robe fell aside at his gentle insistence, baring her body to him. His fingers explored everywhere at once, her breasts, her stomach, the small of her back.

As they finally reached the bed, Tori pulled her lips away and continued tearing at his clothes until she'd stripped him completely. His erection stood tall, exciting her, making her forget everything but him. She walked around him slowly, dodging his hands as he tried to grab for her.

She loved the look of him--the strong curve of his spine, hidden between gloriously smooth muscles. His hips were slender, showcasing his incredible butt. Tori reached forward, touching him, squeezing his cheek lightly. Her stomach tightened. Moisture pooled between her thighs, readying her body for him. She wanted him, always wanted him.

Letting the robe glide off her arms, she shivered as it fell to the floor. She explored his back, his legs, his hips, touching him everywhere. By the time she made her way around, he was panting wildly. His eyes shifted to green in his passion.

Tori placed her finger on his chin and slowly drew it down over his throat. To her surprise, his eyes darkened and his body lurched, tensing as she continued to slide her hand down the middle of his chest. Tilting her head to the side, she watched her finger circle his navel. Heat radiated off his body, stirring her blood. She felt him as if he was already inside of her, part of her.

Quinn's hands lifted as if he would touch her, but he drew them back, letting her take the lead. Tori grinned, moved her hands to his hips, and sank to her knees before him. She flicked her tongue over his hard shaft, playing with the tip until he groaned and begged mindlessly for more.

Her lips wrapped around him, her tongue rolled, her mouth sucked, her teeth grazed. He was too big to fit in her mouth so her hands lifted to help, stroking him, playing with the soft globes she found underneath. Suddenly, he tensed, groaning loud and long, as he held himself back from the edge.

Quinn grabbed her by the arms and lifted her up. A throaty laugh came from her throat as he tossed her easily on the bed. She bounced on the soft mattress.

"You're too much," he growled, crawling over her with a streamlined grace. "You drive me to distraction."

Tori shivered, her body worked up with anticipation. Quinn looked every inch the stalking beast as he came over her. His knees brushed her thighs open and she didn't resist. His strong arms bent slightly at the elbows. He lowered his mouth to take hers, kissing her with a savage heat that consumed her.

He thrust forward, lifting up as he delved inside her. Their shared moans filled the suite. He felt so good, so right. Tori never wanted it to stop. She met his body as he moved within her, confident and sure, gliding in and out of her moistened depths.

His body fell forward so he was lying on top of her, bracing his weight with his elbows. Tori met his kiss. Fingers glided down her body, moving her leg over his shoulder so he could go deeper still.

"Tori," Quinn groaned into her mouth, over and over again.

The tension built. He pumped faster. Her leg looped behind his back, driving him deeper, harder. Tori's back arched off the bed, her body so close to finding fulfillment. She tried to fight it, not wanting the pleasure to stop. With a sudden force that stole her breath and numbed her mind, she climaxed. Her whole being trembled so violently that she was sure the whole planet surely moved with the intensity of it.

"Quinn," she cried, over and over. "Quinn! Quinn! Yes, Quinn!"

Quinn's body couldn't resist the call, as he joined her with his heavy release. His mouth opened, soundless, stretching wide as he drained completely into her body. He was stunned, surprised, frightened--stunned by the force of their joining, surprised by the depth of his feelings, and frightened that he was soon going to lose her.

"Tori," he groaned, wanting to hold onto her forever.

"No," she whispered. "No words. Not tonight. Tonight I can't think. I don't want to feel anything but this, but us. All right, Quinn? Please."

"Yes, nothing but us," he promised, content to pull her tight into his arms as he held her.

"I can't face it," she whispered, her heart aching as she nestled into his strong, protective embrace. She didn't want to leave him, but he hadn't begged her to stay. He hadn't even asked her. And, if he did, she wasn't sure what she would say anyway. "Make love to me again, please, Quinn."

He chuckled softly. "Just try and stop me."

Tori smiled, hiding the sadness under the pleasure he gave her. He made love to her three more times, each release better than the last, until they were too exhausted to move. Sighing in contentment, she fell asleep in his arms.

* * * *

You are mine ... forever. The words were a whisper, spoken from Tori's parted lips. Quinn opened his eyes, waking from a dream. He'd been kissing Tori, making love to her. She was his, completely his. Her dark eyes were staring up at him and she promised to never leave him.

You are mine....

The thought echoed in his brain, a bittersweet torment. Reaching for Tori, he found the bed was empty. He frowned, though he was hardly surprised. She had a habit of sneaking away while he slept. Sitting up, he ran his hand through his hair. Then, slowly, he crawled out of bed, found his clothes, and got dressed.

"Siren," he ordered. "Find Dr. Elliot."

"Good morning, my lord. Dr. Elliot is not in the palace."

"I'm not surprised," he whispered, letting loose a humorless chuckle. Anger built inside him. How dare she go back into the forest without telling him? Quinn surged to his feet and stormed out of the suite.

Her scent was still on his skin. Her voice was in his brain. Quinn growled, feeling his heart like a lead weight in his stomach and he knew he'd never be free of her.

You are mine ... forever.

* * * *

"There is something wrong with me," Quinn announced, walking into the king's office. Kirill looked up from his desk, his dark eye narrowing at the comment. Quinn

swallowed, took a deep breath, and uttered, "I'm ...
broken."

Kirill frowned, standing. His eyes roamed down over his
brother looking for injury. "How do you mean, broken?"

"It will be easier to show you." Quinn's face turned a dark
shade of red and for a long moment, he stood, not moving.
Kirill waited patiently. Finally Quinn sighed and called
over his shoulder, "Come in!"

Kirill's features flooded with confusion, as he watched a
harem woman come into the office. She was very pretty--
young, with dark hair and exotic eyes that could easily
tempt any unmated man. When the woman sighed and
came to stand next to Quinn, a quizzical smile twitched the
corner of the king's mouth. As he watched them, Kirill
moved to lean on the corner of his desk. He didn't say a
word.

"Do it," Quinn ordered the woman, not looking at all
pleased. He didn't care what he looked like. He wasn't
pleased. Tori had ruined him somehow and he wasn't
happy about it. His first impulse had been to run after her
when he discovered she was again missing from his bed,
but pride kept him from going. That was two days ago and
he refused to go crawling back to her. He had to retain
some dignity. He had to forget her. When the woman didn't
move, he said, "Go on. Do it."

The woman frowned, looking dejected. "Again, my lord?
I don't think it will make a difference."

Quinn looked at her. She shrugged. Reaching forward, the
woman grabbed his crotch.

"Ha! See that!" Quinn yelled instantly, as if proving some
point. Kirill merely continued to stare, confused. Ignoring
the woman, the prince pushed her hand aside and waved
her out of the office, "See, broken! She has ruined me!"

"Who? Dr. Elliot?" Kirill asked, realization dawning on
him. He motioned to the harem woman to leave. She
curtsied and obeyed. Quinn ignored her.

"Yes, Dr. Elliot!" Quinn growled, as if the answer was obvious. "She has driven me to madness! I can't eat, can't think. I can't seem to breathe without her in my head! I-I need a cure."

"Quinn, wait," Kirill said in his reasonable older brother tone. Quinn frowned to hear it. He didn't want reason. He wanted to be free of Tori, as she was obviously free of him. "Why ... all this? Has something happened between you and Dr. Elliot? Did you fight? Did she say something?"

"No, she left me without a word! She stole out of my bed, yet again, to run off with those two ... scientists." Quinn slashed his hand through the air in agitation. When he discovered from Reid that the scientists would be gone for a week, camping again in the forest, he'd been livid. Of course, they had an armed guard with them this time and weren't to be left alone, but it didn't matter. He remembered Vitto's words of love. He was a fool to believe she wasn't sleeping with the man.

"You're jealous," Kirill stated, grinning wider. "You're jealous of the male scientists."

"I'm glad my pain amuses you brother," Quinn growled. He felt helpless, not knowing where to go or what to do. All he could think about was her.

"If you are so concerned, why don't you just go out there to see what's going on?"

"And humiliate myself by crawling at her feet?" Quinn had already thought of that, but he didn't think it would work so he saved himself the embarrassment of begging for her to love him.

"Quinn, no--"

"Don't you get it, Kirill? I am not whole!" he cried. Quinn's hands lifted helplessly and his whole frame shook. "Can't you see it? Something has happened to me. I'm ruined, broken, and insane!"

Kirill slowly pushed up from the edge of the desk. His smiled faded. "Quinn, it's all right. Try to calm down. I've never seen you like this."

"You don't understand. I can feel her in me right now. I feel as if I hear her thoughts, but they're unclear. I taste her mouth. I can smell her hair--right now, as I stand before you! My heart beats and it feels her. I want it to stop." The brightness was faded from his eyes as he looked around him. "This is the madness King Attor spoke of. You might have gotten lucky, but not I. I should have heeded our father's warning. I should have stayed clear of her."

"Quinn, you don't--"

"I'm broken," Quinn interrupted, nearing complete desperation. He fell to his knees and buried his face into his hands. His words were muffled, as he hoarsely whispered, "I'm broken, Kirill, and I don't know how to make it go away."

"No, brother, you are not broken," the king said softly. He crossed over to him and placed a hand on his brother's arm. Quinn's eyes rose to meet the king's dark ones. "You are life mated."

Chapter Fourteen

"Tori, this is stupid."

Tori blinked in confusion, looking up at her brother from the ground. The comment came out of nowhere. He held a drill in his hands, waiting as she injected the last of the formula into the last hole. They'd been working for three days, traveling around the marshes, injecting the ground, watching the black moss die a quick death.

Their task had gone a lot smoother than they had at first hoped. Everything looked as if it would be all right. Even the preliminary tests they'd done on the soil looked promising. Within ten years the shadowed marshes should be thriving again with life. There was a deep satisfaction in knowing they had done that.

"What are you talking about?" Tori asked, turning back to her work. "It's a good thing we're doing here. We're saving a planet. We're saving lives. How can you call that stupid?"

Vitto didn't say anything for a long time. Tori turned back to her work. When she finished and moved to push up from the ground, he said, "I'm not talking about our work. I'm talking about you and Prince Quinn. I'm talking about how the two of you are acting like children."

Tori felt the blood drain from her features. Her heart skidded nervously in her chest. She'd been refusing to speak of Quinn since they'd come out to the forest. The morning they had come out to the marshes, she had awakened by his side, shaken to the core by a strange dream. In the dream they were happy and so in love. He promised never to leave her.

You are mine ... forever.

She could still hear his voice in her head, whispering to her. Even now she felt like he was next to her, trying to whisper into her brain. She was terrified that she could feel so much for a man who'd made her no promises. Trying to bury herself in work, she thought to forget him. But, it hadn't worked, not this time. He was always there, ready to torment her thoughts. She could barely eat or sleep and she could very well forget about concentrating on anything more than two seconds at a time.

You are mine ... forever.

She'd looked at Quinn's face, peaceful in sleep as he lay in the bed next to her. His hand had been on her breast, possessively holding her. Tori shivered anew to think of it. She'd been frightened by her feelings, was frightened still.

Tori looked at her hands, pretending to concentrate on dusting them off. It didn't matter, as she was covered in sweat and mud. "What about Prince Quinn? I'm sure I don't know what you're talking about."

"Damn it!" Vitto growled. "Vittoria Rosemary Elliot! So help me you are the most stubborn person I've ever met, or the most stupid!"

"What?" she defended, surprised that Vitto yelled at her in such a tone. He sounded like their father in that moment. "What did I do?"

"They say love is blind, but in your case I'm assuming it's also deaf, dumb, and completely brain dead." Vitto shook his head. "Did you think we wouldn't notice that you ran away from the palace, coming out here to hide?"

"Hide?" Tori shot in return. "I came out here because I had a job to do."

"Hmm, yeah, that's why we found ourselves roused from our beds before dawn to sneak out of the palace--yet again, I might add. You're afraid to face Quinn. Admit it!" Vitto's eyes glared down at her and he didn't give her a chance to answer. "Grant and I have been waiting for you to work whatever nonsense is in your head out, but I give up. If you're not going to call a spade a spade, then I'll have to say it for you. I know you, Tor. I've known you my whole life. You know I love you and always will. We're family. And that's why I can say this to you. You're being a stupid ass. You need to stop being so involved in your work and you need to concentrate on you. You're in love with him, Tori. You're in love with Prince Quinn."

"But, Vitto--"

"No buts!" Vitto growled. Tori jolted in surprise. She'd never seen him like this. "I'll not watch you throw your life away because you're too stupid to see the answer that is right in front of you. More often than not, the simplest solution to a problem is the right one."

Tori's mouth trembled, as she fought to hold back her tears. "Vitto, I know you mean well, but you don't understand. What I feel is one sided."

Vitto snorted, looking like he was about to argue. She held up her hand.

"Please, Vitto, don't make this harder on me. He's made me no promises," Tori swallowed.

"Have you given him a reason to?" Vitto asked, drawing her forward into his embrace. "I know how you are. You're safe, cautious. You'll only proceed when the answer is clear. As a scientist, that little characteristic is great. As a woman, it just plain sucks. He probably had to tell you fifty times that he was attracted to you before you'd sleep with him."

Tori turned bright red. Quinn had said he wanted her several times before she'd finally given in, even though she'd wanted him just as badly from the very beginning. Vitto was right. She did play it safe.

"Men are stubborn creatures and these men are more so than others. I was talking to Reid and from what I gathered about their upbringing, their father wasn't exactly the best teacher. They weren't lucky like we were. We had parents who loved us openly, and knew how to express it with and without words. Quinn and his brothers weren't raised to recognize emotions like love. And if he can't recognize it, why do you think he would know how to express it?"

Tori shivered. Vitto's words made sense. King Attor had been a horrible man, an unworthy father--unloving, murderous, a tyrant. Quinn did have a strong sense of duty and commitment to his people. But, aside from Kirill with his wife, she'd never seen any of the brothers confess or show that they cared for each other--at least not openly so. The respect and closeness was there, but she doubted any of them knew how to express what they felt with words.

Tori and Vitto had been raised in a home where love was so openly spoken that she'd grown to take it for granted. She'd been sitting around, waiting for Quinn to openly say how he felt for her, to just come out and tell her. Remembering the queen's words, she sighed. Ulyssa had told her that sometimes it takes a knock to the head to get the Var men to confess anything. She'd told her to ask Quinn straight out what he felt for her. Why hadn't she listened to her advice? Who better to know than a woman who managed to break through Attor's demented teachings?

"Vitto, I have to go," Tori whispered. She handed him her equipment. Almost in a daze, she backed away. "I have to go."

"Wait, Tori, you can't leave yet," Vitto said, stepping after her.

She froze, looking at him in question. "But, you just said I should ... I have to tell him how I feel."

"Um, that's great, Tor," Vitto said. "But, as a man, can I give you one little bit more advice?"

"What? Anything?" Tori's round eyes looked up at him as he came to her. His eyes moved briefly over her clothes.

Vitto grinned, a mischievous glint in his brotherly eyes. "Take a bath first and get cleaned up. You smell like a pig sty."

Tori's mouth fell open and she glanced down at her muddied clothes. She did look a frightful mess. Vitto's hand lifted to her face and he pushed her mouth shut with one finger.

"Water's that way," he said, pointing to where the water container sat in one of the tents. "I'll get the camp packed up while you get cleaned up."

* * * *

Tori's whole body jolted with nervous excitement. The walk back to the palace seemed like it took forever. She stayed quiet, lost in thought as she rehearsed what she would say in her head. She hardly paid attention to the large trees or the red earthen path. Several times she began to walk off course, deep in thought. Vitto or Grant would reach out and pull her back, not bothering to say a word to her about it as they shot her impish grins. The men chatted next to her, going back and forth with their Var escorts.

Her heart pounded furiously as she neared the palace. She was sure her face was flooded with the heat of her nervousness. Tori swallowed, trying to still her shaking limbs. Suddenly, she stopped. Turning to Vitto, she whispered, "What if he says nothing?"

"Trust me, Tori. He'll say something." Vitto took her gently by the arm and almost had to drag her to get her to move forward. "If you don't take the chance, you'll never forgive yourself. At least this way, you'll know for sure how he feels."

Tori thought about Vitto's words and before she realized it, he'd dragged her to the banquet hall. A few Var soldiers sat about the tables, drinking and joking. Half eaten plates of food were set before them. At their entrance, the noise lessened as several turned to look at the newly returned scientists.

"Hey, guys, I'm going to take a bath and find Linzi. I'll see you later," Grant said, glancing into the hall but not entering it. "Elliot, I expect a full report."

Tori nodded weakly, barely hearing the man. She looked around, ignoring the stares. At the head table was Quinn. He sat next to his brothers. When her eyes found his, she didn't see anything else. She stared for a long moment. She felt faint. She couldn't do it.

Turning to Vitto, who still held her arm, she whispered, "There are too many people here. I can't do this!"

"You can," Vitto answered, placing two hands on her shoulders. "I know he cares for you, Tori. I've seen the way he looks at you."

"But--"

"No buts," Vitto ordered. "Or I'll kick you in yours."

Tori chuckled softly at the look he gave her. He was right. It was time to tell Quinn how she felt about him, how much she loved him, how she never wanted to take another breath without him by her side.

* * * *

Quinn watched Tori walk into the hall with Vitto. He had to blink several times to make sure the vision was real. They hadn't been expecting them back so soon. The guards that had escorted them walked into the hall, going immediately to the tables to join their comrades. Grant poked his head in, said something to Tori and Vitto and then disappeared.

He watched through narrowed eyes as Vitto grabbed Tori by the shoulders. His hand gripped tightly around his goblet in jealousy. When Tori laughed, a rage ripped through him and he couldn't contain his anger any longer. Slamming down the goblet, he stood. All eyes turned to him.

"Get your hands off of her!" Quinn demanded, glaring at Vitto.

Several of the men gasped, turning to look at Vitto and Tori. Vitto slowly let her go. Kirill hid his grin behind his hand. Ulyssa did the same.

"What are you doing?" Reid hissed, trying to get Quinn's attention.

"Quiet, Reid," the bandaged Falke ordered at his side. Reid blinked in annoyance at the command, but said no more.

Tori's eyes finally left his and she glanced around the quiet hall. Quinn could see her hands tremble from his place at the head table. He hadn't meant to scare her. Coming around the platform, he marched forward.

"Prince Quinn," Vitto said. "Perhaps there has been a misunderstanding."

"I choose Tori as mine. You are not to touch her." Quinn announced. His words were so tense that they echoed harshly over the banquet hall for all to hear. There were several more gasps and a loud murmur of excited whispers.

"What?" Tori whispered, her eyes round in disbelief. "What?"

"Do not deny that you are mine," he growled, not caring who heard. "Everyone here can see how you want me. My scent is all over you. You belong to me."

Tori paled, not sure if she should be mortified or not by the bold statement. On a base level she felt pleasure in his possessive words. She glanced at Vitto and then at Quinn. Her mouth opened but no sound came out, as she desperately looked around the hall for help. Slowly, as if in a fog, she saw Kirill stand up and begin to move toward them.

"Quinn," the king said softly, gently touching his brother's stiff arm. "Why don't you take Dr. Elliot for a walk? You're making a scene."

Quinn didn't even look at him. He stalked forward, grabbed Tori's arm, and dragged her from the hall without stopping to ask her if she wanted to go. Tori stumbled in stunned silence as he led her to his wing of the palace. He tossed her inside his home and slammed the door shut. Her feet slid across the smooth tile floor, nearly tripping on the raised platform holding the couch. Slowly, she righted herself. She glanced around, getting her bearings. Her eyes moved over the tall decorative arches of his home, and finally landed on the thick wall of glass guarding the bathroom.

She shivered. There was no where to run if things turned for the worse. Quinn was acting strange. Very carefully, she turned to study him. He made a move to touch her and she jerked back.

"Quinn?" Tori panted. His show of fury aroused her, but she held back from him, not understanding. "You're scaring me. What's going on?"

"I thought I could handle your and," he paused, his face contorting in disgust as he spat, "*Vitto's* relationship, but I can't. You have to choose, Tori. Him or me. You can't have both."

"Vitto?"

The word barely escaped her lips when Quinn pounced forward to grab her arms. He shook her lightly, not hurting her. "Damn it, Tori! You don't love him. You ... can't love him."

"Wait," Tori panted, shaking her head. "I do love him, of course I love him. He's--"

Quinn let her go and slowly backed away shaking his head in denial. His heart felt as if it was being ripped from his chest. He wasn't sure he'd be able to control himself. "You'd better leave then, quickly."

"Quinn, listen--"

"Leave!" he shouted. "Go!"

Tori began to move toward the door and stopped. Her voice rising, she turned back to him and growled, "No, you just shut up for a second! I've got something to say and so help me if you don't let me say it I'll-I'll...."

Quinn's brow lifted, impatiently urging her to get on with it. His chest heaved as he fought to control himself. Tori wasn't scared, she was frustrated.

"I'll hit you over the head until you see reason or get knocked unconscious!" Tori yelled. Quinn didn't move.

His lips twitched at the corner as if he would smile at her threat. "Damn it. I had this speech all prepared. It was perfect. But then you had to go act like a meathead so I can't remember what I was going to say. We're adults and we're acting like children or was it that we're being children. Give me a second. I know it was something like that."

"Meathead?" Quinn broke into her thoughts. "Did you actually call me a meathead?

"Well, you are. Oh, never mind that. I'm trying to..." A small sound of aggravation left her throat. She couldn't remember what she was going to say. Then, unable to keep it in any longer, she blurted, "I'm in love with you."

Quinn didn't move. His eyes brightened slightly as he studied her. His mouth opened but nothing came out.

"Okay? That's what I wanted to tell you. I'm in love with you and," she hesitated, unsure whether she wanted to throw her arms around him or run for the door screaming. Nothing came out the way she meant it. She wanted to say other things--give him a long list of why she loved him, of why they could work together, of why he should give them a chance. All those reasons left her as she looked at him. How could she explain everything she felt? Instead, she whispered, "I love you, Quinn. I love you."

She shrugged helplessly, waiting for him to speak. Every inch of her shook, as she waited for his reaction. If he didn't return her love, she wasn't sure she'd be able to survive it.

"You can't have us both," he answered softly. The very look of him took her breath away and stole her heart. "I can't share you, Tori. Please, don't ask me to."

"What?" Tori whispered, confused. "What are you...?"

"Vitto. You can't have us both." Quinn stepped for her. His hand lifted to gently touch her cheek. He caressed her with his strong fingers, sending chills over her flesh.

"What are you talking about?" Tori took heart in the fact that he was touching her. That was a good sign, wasn't it? His hand felt warm against her skin, making her tremble to be in his arms. "Quinn, Vitto's my younger brother. We were both named after our father. When I say I love him, it's because he's my family. Of course I love him. He's Vitto Elliot. I'm Vittoria Elliot. We don't really announce the fact that we're related because we have to work together and it's caused problems for us in the past. So he's Dr. Vitto and I'm Dr. Elliot. Did you really think that he was my...?"

Tori began to laugh, unable to even say the words out loud. She knew he'd thought Vitto was a threat to her at one point, but she really thought he'd gotten over it. I mean, even if he wasn't her brother, it was Vitto.

"He's your brother?" Quinn asked, needlessly. His face darkened.

"I just assumed you'd been told," Tori answered. "Naturally, the king--"

"Kirill knew?" Quinn demanded, his expression darkening even more in his annoyance.

"Of course he did," Tori said. "He was told when we arrived. He had our records. I thought everyone knew. Reid, Falke--"

"They know as well?" Quinn interrupted. He frowned. Trust his brothers to watch him squirm. Damn Kirill! When Quinn had told him that he suspected Tori and Vitto were lovers, the king had sat there grinning at him like a fool-- saying nothing.

"It came up in the forest on our way to Myrddin's. We were telling childhood stories while you were on your walk. They wanted to know why Vitto and I seemed to know each other so well." Tori shrugged. Her hand lifted to touch his solid chest, running the tips of her fingers lightly over the muscular folds. Then, licking her lips, her eyes lit with hope, as she asked, "Does this mean you were jealous over me?"

Quinn pulled her into his arms, his bright blue eyes piercing down into hers. Tori lifted her arms up around his neck. She offered her lips to him.

"Yes," he whispered, leaning down to kiss her softly. His lips brushed along hers. "I was jealous over you, woman."

Tori sighed, her whole being filled with emotion and anticipation. She twined her fingers through his light brown hair, studying it intently for a moment. "And does this mean you maybe care for me just a little?"

Quinn rubbed his nose along hers, pulling her so close she could feel his arousal pressing into her stomach. When he spoke, his lips moved along hers. "Yes, how can you not know that I love you? I've loved you from the first moment I saw you. There hasn't been anyone else since I met you. I confess, at one point I tried to get you out of my system, when I didn't think you cared. But, I couldn't do it. No other woman can hold a candle to you, Tori. I love you."

Tori panted. It was the sweetest thing anyone had ever said to her. Her eyes dipped to the side, shy. "And does this mean you maybe want me to stay here with you?"

"It would be strange for a wife to leave her husband," Quinn murmured.

Tori moaned, barely hearing his words as his mouth continued to do delicious things to her senses. His kiss deepened, as his tongue moved forward to explore deeper. She felt him all the way to her toes. It was perfect and she knew she belonged forever in his arms. Then, as what he said sunk in, she pulled back. "Did you say wife? Are you asking me to life mate with you?"

"No, not asking," Quinn answered, leaning forward to steal her breath as his hand roamed down over her body. "I'm afraid you don't have a choice in the matter, Dr. Elliot. You are my wife."

"Is that a royal command, Prince Quinn?" she teased, feeling giddy and so very happy. His body felt so right against hers. "Are you saying I have no choice but to marry you?"

"Ah, yeah, well not really," Quinn chuckled. "I can't ask you to do what has already been done."

"What do you mean?" Tori stiffened in his arms, her throat dry. She didn't dare move.

"Our souls mated the first night we were together," Quinn answered. His hand grew bolder and she let go of a small moan. Slowly, he peeled back her clothing, baring her body to him. "It just took our heads and our hearts a little while to catch up."

"But, how is that possible?" Tori sighed, her eyes closing as he kissed her neck.

Tori, listen to me, she heard whispered in her brain. It was Quinn's voice and it tugged at her memory. *You are mine.*

Mmmm, all right Quinn, yours, she vaguely recalled herself to answer him.

The memory was like a distant dream, Quinn telling her that she was his and she agreeing. Looking up at him, she saw he was remembering it to. At the time, she'd thought he meant sexually, as a conquest. Now, she finally understood. How could she not have realized it sooner? His words and her sleepy agreement to them had sealed them forever. That is why neither one of them had felt whole since. They were two pieces of the same being. He was her husband, her mate, her entire life. The beauty of its simplicity washed through her. "I didn't know you. I--"

"I told you once before," Quinn murmured into her flesh. His breathing became hard pants as he began to slowly make love to her. He bit her earlobe, causing her to whimper. "The Var don't put much stock in ceremony. All it takes is the will of two people and it is done. We couldn't have mated if we both didn't want it. You are mine, Tori, and I am yours. Forever."

Tori grabbed his face in her hands and pulled his mouth hard to hers. Nothing else mattered. She was finally home. Quinn lifted her up in his arms and walked her to the long pillows thrown across the floor before the fireplace. Setting her on the floor, he stripped her completely of her clothing.

His eyes roamed down over her skin, stopping to look at her large breasts. Soon his clothes were also tossed aside. Loudly, he commanded, "Fire."

A fire lit in the fireplace. Quinn picked up their clothes and threw them in. Tori gasped. "What are you doing?"

"I figure if you don't have anything to wear, you can't escape me. Tomorrow, when I wake up, you're going to be right by my side." Quinn swept forward, only to lower her down to the long pillows on the floor. His body pressed into hers, rocking the heavy mass between his legs with slow intent along her naked hip. With a devilish glint in his eyes, he whispered, "So, when you said, 'saddle up cowboy' what did this mean? I admit to being very curious about it."

Tori turned a light shade of pink. "Cowboys are part of old earth culture. They used to ride on top of wild horses. It's a saying now."

Quinn chuckled at her look. "Mm, I like this game already. Tell me more. Who will ride whom?"

Tori just grinned, flipping him on his back. She moved to straddle his waist, lifting her ready body to accept his heavy length inside her, where he belonged. "It would be much better if I just showed you."

Tori lowered her body down onto his shaft, letting him fill her. Moving up and down, she saw his eyes watching her in adoration. They made love before the fire twice before moving to the bedroom. Neither one of them spoke, not needing to as their minds were joined with just one thought, *you are mine ... forever.*

* * * *

Tori sighed, looking over Quinn and her home. It had been three glorious weeks since she moved in with him and she couldn't have been happier. Pulling the robe around her shoulders, she wished for a brief second that her husband would stop burning all her clothes. Not once had she tried to sneak out while he slept. She knew he trusted her, but just had to assume that he got some sort of masculine pleasure by keeping her naked all the time and ready for him.

Hearing a knock on the door, she looked over from the fireplace and grinned. "Come in!"

Ulyssa opened the door, smiling. In her arms, she carried a bundle of clothing. "I thought you might need these. I see that I was right."

Tori chuckled, nodding. "Thanks."

Ulyssa tossed the clothes on the low couch next to Tori and sat down across from her on a big floor pillow. The queen politely averted her eyes as Tori got dressed. Tori sighed, pulling the shirt over her head and the pants over her hips. It fit snug against her breasts, but she didn't care. She knew Quinn got much enjoyment from seeing the tight material binding her down. He liked freeing her from it even more--kind of like rescuing them. She hid her chuckle.

"Not that I care if you borrow my clothes," Ulyssa said, "but I'm starting to run low. Can't Quinn tie you to the bed or something if he's so worried about you leaving while he sleeps?"

Tori and Ulyssa had become really good friends, as well as sisters, over the past weeks. It was nice to have another human woman to talk to about things. For the most part life was perfect, but their husbands were still Var and caused their wives moments of pure frustration.

"He has," Tori blushed, thinking about how carefree and inventive her husband had been since they finally proclaimed their love for each other. In no time at all, all traces of the moody prince were gone, leaving her the playful man she'd fallen in love with. And, oh, was he playful. The things that man could come up with in the bedroom left her blushing and breathless. Knowing he'd shared his life with her, and she was going to live for several hundred years had been a shock at first, but she knew she'd never get bored with him.

"I see," Ulyssa said, glancing around the hall and pausing as she studied the front door. A small smile graced her pretty features. "Have you told him? I haven't heard any announcements."

"Oh," Tori blushed. Ulyssa had seen her at the medics the day before. "I wanted to be sure first."

"Sure of what?" Quinn asked, his voice directly behind her, his lips close to her neck. Tori yelped in surprise and jumped slightly as she spun around in her seat. His eyes roamed over her body and he frowned. Looking at Ulyssa, he grumbled, "Why'd you bring more clothes for her? I liked what she had on."

"She's going to have to leave this room today and I don't need a naked woman roaming the palace halls. You Var men are sexually charged as it is. We'd have a riot amongst the guards. Oh, and Quinn, your brother commands you--as your king--to stop burning all your wife's clothing."

"He does?" Quinn asked, looking perplexed. "Why would he care? I am paying for them and can burn them if I wish."

"He'll care as soon as I tell him to care." Ulyssa giggled and winked at Tori. "I'm the only other women in this place who doesn't live in the harem and I'll be damned if you're going to keep her locked in here all the time. Tori don't let this man distract you. I have merchants coming and I want to ... you know, shop for stuff together. If you don't show up in the banquet hall in twenty minutes, I'm sending in the guards and having Quinn arrested for disobeying a royal order--at least for the afternoon."

Tori nodded, giggling even as she blushed slightly. When Ulyssa was gone, Quinn jumped over the back of the couch and pulled her into her arms. Kissing her thoroughly, he said, "Shopping? What is it I'm not being told?"

"Ulyssa and I are going to spend all of your and Kirill's money," Tori teased. Her hands ran lovingly over his shoulders and chest, patting down his tunic shirt. "And I'm buying a whole new wardrobe--two in fact."

"Ah, come on, I like the one you've got." Quinn tugged at her shirt laces, working the top out just enough so he could look down her shirt at her cleavage. His hand came up over the material and cupped a soft globe, watching as the motion pushed the cleavage up toward his face. "Mm, I love your breasts. They're so soft."

"I don't have a wardrobe," Tori reminded him, swallowing as a wave of pleasure came over her. "I don't have clothes."

"I know," he groaned, moving his lips down to kiss a top curve of a breast as his hand pushed it up. His thumb rolled over the clothed nipple. "That's what I like about it."

"But, I didn't mean just for me," Tori said carefully. "The second wardrobe is for someone else."

"Hmm," Quinn sighed, paying more attention to the angle of her nipple to his tongue. Tori shivered under his mouth as he tried his best to reach it by dipping beneath the shirt. Then, as if he lost his train of thought, said absently, "I don't care. Spend as much money as you wish. You can have anything your heart desires."

"Good. Because the other wardrobe is for the baby," she whispered.

"Mm, all right," he murmured, his tongue finally reaching the aching bud. Suddenly, he stopped, his tongue froze on her nipple before slowly being drawn back into his mouth. His words muffled by her chest, he said very carefully, "Baby? Kirill's baby?"

"Um, it better not be his baby," Tori teased, running her hand over his arms. "I'm sure I'd remember--"

Quinn's mouth crushing into hers cut off her words. When he'd kissed her long and hard, he pulled back grinning. His hand strayed to her stomach. Merriment lit his bright blue gaze, as he teased, "So, this means you're breasts are going to get even bigger, right? And more tender? I like that."

"Ah!" Tori feigned outrage as she hit his arms. "Quinn!"

"What?" He grinned, kissing her again, this time tender and soft. "I love you, wife."

"I love you," Tori mumbled, still eyeing him ruefully.

In one artful pull, he had her on her back on the couch and her shirt pulled up over her stomach. He sprinkled light feathery kisses over her. "And I love you, too, my son."

"Son?" Tori asked. "It could be a girl."

"Possibly," Quinn chuckled, humoring her. "But, girl children are rare here. You know that."

"Don't remind me that I'll always be outnumbered by Var men." Tori chuckled.

Quinn looked up, concerned. "Do you mind having sons?"

"If they are yours, how can I not love having them?" Tori stroked back his hair. "Now, get off me so I can go baby shopping with the queen. Though, I have to admit, seeing you tied down in chains does hold some appeal."

To Tori's surprise, Quinn kissed her quickly and jumped to his feet. She sat up, stunned. He rushed to the door. "I'm going to go tell everyone."

Her mouth fell open as he left her. Just as she was standing to right her clothes, his head popped in around the corner. A big, silly grin was spread over his excited features. He'd never looked more handsome, or more proud. "I love you, wife."

"I love you, too. Go, tell the world. I'll see you later tonight so we can finish this." Tori shook her head as he went to do just that. Sighing she moved after him, hearing his shouts of joy coming from the end of the hall. Whispering, she said with a laugh, "I love you, too, husband."

* * * *

Tori looked around her home in amazement. One day. It had only taken Quinn only one day to buy enough stuff for ten children and she was barely a month along. Working her way through the boxes she chuckled and set down her small shopping bag of baby clothes. It looked pitifully small compared to the furniture and mounds of clothing set before her.

"There you are!" Quinn beamed proudly at her, walking in the front door. "I was looking for you. Ulyssa said you came back here, so I must have just missed you in the hall."

"I've see you've been busy," Tori laughed. She watched her husband wade through the boxes and bags to reach her. It took awhile, but he'd finally made it to her side. Stopping, he kissed her soundly then leaned over to her belly to do the same. "Do you really think we need all this stuff? It's just one baby."

"Only one now. I plan on keeping you with my children for many years to come." Quinn grinned, nuzzling her now bare stomach with light kisses. His voice became hoarse, rasping, as he admitted, "I shall enjoy watching your body grow round with my sons."

Quinn made a low growling sound as if the mere thought of her pregnant body aroused him. Tori wasn't so sure that it sounded like a good plan to her, but merely said, "Let's get through number one first and then we'll talk about the others."

"We'll build onto this wing. I think at least twelve sons," Quinn continued, as if he hadn't heard her. "Maybe more. Sixteen has a nice ring to it."

"Sixteen?" Tori squeaked. She was still trying to get used to the idea of one.

Before he could answer a knock sounded on the door. Quinn pulled back up, covering her stomach from view. His hand lingering on her possessively, before yelling, "Come in!"

Tori watched in awe as Kirill, Reid, and Falke struggled to bring in the most hideous stuffed creature she'd ever seen. Quinn kissed her temple and went to go help. The strange beast was twice as tall as the men and had the spine of an earth porcupine along its thick back, looking as sharp as razor blades. His head was just as vicious with long deadly fangs and eyes that looked eerie even in its taxidermy state.

It was a struggle getting it through the door and when they finally managed, they set it up in the living room. The horrible beast stared down at her, looking altogether the thing nightmares were made of. The four brothers watched her proudly, as she looked at the awful thing. Vaguely, she was aware of her jaw hanging open in stunned silence.

"Ah," Kirill said to Quinn, slapping him in the chest with a big grin. "Look at her face, she loves it!"

"How can she not?" Quinn answered and got instant nods of agreement from his brothers. "I told you earth women liked stuffed creatures."

"Quinn?" Tori asked, weak. "What is this thing?"

"A Yorkin," Falke supplied. He still moved stiffly from being tortured by Lord Myrddin, but he was too proud to let it show. Tori felt bad for him. He'd really been hurt the worst out of all of them. She couldn't begin to imagine the horror he'd been through. "We took it down ourselves last year in a hunt--it only took the four of us to defeat it."

"Yes," Tori said. "I'm afraid I still don't understand."

"Well," Reid explained as if it should've been perfectly clear. "Quinn told us of the baby and for a gift, he said you'd like either flowers--which he's already picked all of them and given to you--or hunted offerings. None of us know of this fearsome teddy bear you speak of, but we are sure this creature has to be at least twice as deadly as one."

Tori's jaw dropped further. She wanted to laugh, but their faces were so earnest, so proud of what they'd given her, she couldn't bring herself to say anything.

"What in the...?" Ulyssa said from the door.

"They've brought me a beast more fearsome than a teddy bear," Tori said. She'd confessed the misunderstanding to Ulyssa one night who hadn't breathed a word of it.

"Oh," Ulyssa said, and Tori saw her struggling not to smile. Turning to her husband, she winked and said, "It's almost as good as the weapons you all gave me for the baby."

The four Vars' grins deepened.

"Good God!" Vitto exclaimed coming in. Grant was next to him. "What is that thing?"

"A Yorkin," Quinn supplied, waving to encompass the beast.

Vitto smiled at Tori. He gave an amused glance around at all the boxes.

"Are you giving birth to an army?" Grant asked, laughing as he too looked around.

"Not yet," Quinn supplied. "But, soon."

Ulyssa shot her a pointed look. Tori just shrugged weakly and helplessly shook her head.

"Um, Lyssa...?" Kirill began.

"Ah, no. No army for you, my king," Ulyssa automatically answered. "Maybe three."

"But..." the king said, looking as if his wife took away his favorite toy. He glanced meaningfully at Tori and Quinn. "Quinn--"

"We'll discuss it later," Ulyssa said, smiling lovingly at him.

"Fine." The king actually looked like he pouted.

Reid frowned slightly in discomfort and looked to the floor. He always seemed to stiffen up whenever any of his brothers acted affectionate toward their wives. She knew that being raised by Attor had scarred each of them more than they'd ever admit. She only hoped that someday Reid and Falke would both find the happiness they had. Oh, and Jarek, she mustn't forget her other new brother--the space explorer.

Vitto made his way through the boxes to hand her a small stuffed bear he carried. Grinning at her, he said, "I hate leaving. I promise to come back after my next assignment and see you."

"Me, too," Grant said. Tori knew they were both signed up with the HIA for another mission. It seemed they both enjoyed the danger that working for human intelligence brought. She worried about them, but knew they were smart, capable men. She had finished her work, sending her reports in to ESC and HIA over a week ago. Dr. Simon's belongings went with it. HIA mission director, Franklin, said he'd make sure it got to Dr. Simon's family.

Handing her the bear, Vitto said, "I know it's just a teddy bear, but I wanted the baby to have something from his uncle before I left."

At Vitto's words, Tori heard a round of gasps. All four Var warriors made their way through the boxes to see the small bear. Quinn took it from Tori's hands and examined it. Reid grabbed it from him and did the same, passing it on to Falke and Kirill.

"Where are its teeth?" Quinn asked, frowning, not at all impressed by the small furry animal.

"It's so small," Reid said. "Is it poisonous? Does it shift?"

"We could easily hunt this," Falke added. "It has no claws. Were they perhaps removed?"

"Does it have fangs? Is it spry?" Quinn asked. He pulled at the stuffed animal's mouth, but couldn't get it open to see.

Kirill lifted the bear and sniffed it before turning to his wife. Holding it up, he said, "Lyssa, you are frightened by this thing?"

The four humans began to laugh. The Var looked them over, confused.

"Come on, guys," Ulyssa said, ushering them out. "Let's leave these two alone. Vitto, Grant, come help me explain."

Once alone, Tori eyed the Yorkin. No matter how misguided, it really was sweet of her new family. She turned to her husband. He held the bear, poking at its soft, fake fur in confusion. She leaned over and kissed him soundly.

Pulling back, he again eyed the bear in severe concentration, and said, "I could have hunted this on my own, without my brothers. You know that, don't you? I will get you one if you truly wish for me to find one."

"I know you could have, sweetheart, I know." Tori grinned. It was so sweet that he was worried his Yorkin disappointed her compared to the bear Vitto gave her. She pushed him back through the boxes to their bedroom, her hands roaming beneath his clothes.

"That Yorkin took five days to track and we fought for nearly three hours to bring it down. Usually it takes at least twenty men twice as long. It supplied meat for the whole palace for months." Quinn didn't seem to notice that he was already half naked, but as she pulled off her shirt and threw it on the bear in his hand, he glanced up. A grin instantly spread over his features.

"Mm, yes, you're my big bad hunter, aren't you?" Tori said, playfully pushing him back. "Why don't you come show me how you *track your prey*?"

Quinn's eyes flashed with the threat of a shift, sending hot arousal through her. He instantly dropped the bear but held onto the shirt. Lifting his wife over his shoulder, he rushed her to the bedroom. He laid her gently on the bed and undressed her completely. When they were both naked, he yelled, "Fire!"

"Oh, no, Quinn!" Tori protested, watching her clothes fly toward the fireplace. "Not again!"

"I disobeyed a royal decree, wife." Quinn kissed her. "Now, wasn't there some sort of punishment due me? Something to do with chains?"

"Mm, you're such an outlaw," she moaned.

Quinn grinned, chuckling as he covered her body with his, easing his thighs between her legs. Tori's laughter joined his and her arms wrapped around his solid neck, not caring if she ever wore clothes again.

THE END

To learn more about the Lords of the Var series, or Michelle M Pillow's other titles, please visit her website (www.michellepillow.com).

Printed in the United States
62936LVS00013B/148-270